The
PHANTOM
of
PENN
STATION

The
PHANTOM
of
PENN
STATION

A Novel

Mike Monahan

Book Cover by Gary Val Tenuta

Book Editor Lorraine Fico-White, Magnifico Manuscripts

Book Design and Ebook Conversion
by Lorie DeWorken, MIND the MARGINS, LLC

ISBN 13: 978-0-692-14836-5 (paperback)

First Edition

Printed in the United States of America

Also by Mike Monahan

Barracuda

Mutant barracuda wreaks havoc at the grand opening of the Majestic Hotel/Casino Dive Center on Bikini Island.

Barracuda II
The Return

If you thought the mutant barracuda from *Barracuda* was horrifying, wait until you find out what's in store in the sequel! *Barracuda II: The Return* is a crime thriller and horror story, all rolled into one suspense-filled action adventure.

Barracuda III
The Final Conflict

In the wake of a devastating earthquake and tsunami, Japan must deal with growing ecological threats as familiar faces reunite to recover priceless artifacts from Yakuza thieves.

The Treasure of Hart Island

Hart Island is haunted by the spirits of the dead. It is used as a potter's field for indigenous peoples, each grave dug by the convicts on nearby Rikers Island. Underneath its sandy shores lie bones and death.

It also holds a secret.

"Bleak, dark, and piercing cold, it was a night for the well-housed and fed to draw round the bright fire, and thank God they were at home; and for the homeless starving wretch to lay him down and die. Many hunger-worn outcasts close their eyes in our bare streets at such times, who, let their crimes have been what they may, can hardly open them in a more bitter world."

—Charles Dickens

CHAPTER

1

"Franklin, I want you to take Tiny to work with you today. I have to clean the house and set up the Christmas decorations."

"Dee, I thought you wanted the boy to help you bring the decorations from the garage into the house?"

"No! I don't want that idiot under my feet and getting in my way."

Franklin Wilson let out a quiet sigh. He was tired from all the overtime he put in with the Metropolitan Transit Authority (MTA). A tenured brakeman who had already done his time riding the rails, he now worked exclusively coupling and uncoupling trains in Penn Station when he wasn't throwing track switches.

He hated it when his wife of twenty-seven years called their son an idiot. Sure, Tobias was mentally slower than other twenty-five-year-olds, but he was as big and strong as an ox. Tobias had to be homeschooled by Franklin and Dee because he was bullied in school, despite his size. One time Tobias defended himself from a group of bullies and sent them to the hospital. The school overlooked the incident but had a zero tolerance for hospitalizing such bullies.

Franklin's brother, Charlie, nicknamed Tobias Tiny when he was a big ten-year-old child. The name stuck.

Franklin enjoyed taking his son to work with him. Tiny had a great interest in the railroad and all of its exciting underground features. Franklin mostly worked alone and Tiny was unsociable, so the relationship worked well.

As a longtime MTA employee, Franklin knew of all the hidden underground tunnels and deserted railroad platforms far beneath the hustle and bustle of Penn Station. His son was fascinated by these historic relics that most people weren't aware of.

Each time the pair went to work, Franklin brought Tiny to another secret location between jobs.

"Always keep an eye out for the Mole People," his father warned.

"Why are they called that?" Tiny asked.

"They live deep underground in abandoned tunnels, buildings, and corridors. They suffer from a multitude of mental, social, and environmental problems, so keep your distance."

Tiny's eyes widened in amazement, even though he didn't completely understand.

Franklin backed the family's Toyota Rav-4 out of the narrow driveway as Tiny stood on the street corner. All of the homes on this serene suburban street were adorned with colorful Christmas decorations. Today Dee would decorate theirs.

The two drove from their quaint, tree-lined street down the West Side Highway into Manhattan and entered the 34th Street Hudson Yards. Parking the car, the pair skipped the short bus ride to Penn Station and walked.

It was a cool brisk morning and everyone was caught up in the NYC charm at Christmas time. Franklin needed the icy air to clear his head since he worked late the night before doing unscheduled couplings of deadhead subway trains.

As the father and son approached the entrance to Penn Station, Franklin said, "Come over to this alley. I'll show you another way to enter the lower levels."

Franklin pulled out a huge key ring and searched for the correct key, then opened a small, rusty door hidden between two commercial premises. The door screeched as the vintage hinges awoke from their long, deep slumber of inactivity.

Silently they entered a dark, clammy, cobblestone-lined corridor. Franklin pulled out a flashlight from his coat pocket and shined it before them.

Tiny was as giddy with excitement as he was with fear. He loved these ancient passageways that hadn't been used in many years. He may not have been book smart, but he learned a lot about the catacombs beneath the city.

They walked through giant boiler rooms and ancient hallways until they reached the MTA workers' locker room. Franklin changed into his work overalls and grabbed a large tool bag. He checked the work roster assigned to him and saw the first job was to uncouple Subway Car # 24243 from a line of deadheads located in a discontinued Interborough Rapid Transit Company (IRT) line at 34th Street and Ninth Avenue.

He smiled broadly as he led his son in the direction of the job site.

"Tiny, let me tell you about this particular railroad tunnel we are going to. We will be several levels beneath the grimy streets of New York. This station was demolished in 1940, but the tunnels and tracks still remain. Deadhead cars are stored here until they are either pulled out to be destroyed, repaired, or returned to service."

He stopped to adjust his heavy tool bag and continued. "The station had two levels. The lower level contained two tracks and two side platforms. The upper level had one track and two side platforms. The trains ran southbound, first to 30th Street, then down to 14th Street."

Tiny wasn't too interested in his father's dramatic monologue about the history of abandoned stations. He was more interested in the layout of the tracks, alleys, corridors, and strange rooms that lined the vintage subway tubes. This was his version of Disneyland.

Soon they reached the deserted track, and Franklin placed his heavy tool bag on the ground and pulled out his work order. The work locomotive that would remove the trains was parked directly in front of a string of twelve derelict subway cars.

Franklin walked along the chain of ancient train cars and spotted #24243. It was fourth in line. He would uncouple #24243, and the locomotive would remove the string of four cars to the Sunnyside Queens maintenance yards for evaluation.

The engineer was not in the cab of the engine, so he yelled to his son, "Tiny, go into that comfort station over there and tell the engineer that I am here!"

Tiny entered the dusty remnants of a recreational room for railroad employees to rest between jobs.

"Hi, Mr. Collins," he said.

An older, weary-looking gent was eating his breakfast at a small table and quickly looked up. "Well, hello to you, Tiny."

Tiny smiled at the old man, enjoying the use of his nickname by the people he liked. "Dad's outside."

"OK, tell him to finish the uncoupling while I finish my meal, then he can couple my engine to the string of four. I'll take you for a ride out to the Sunnyside repair terminal. How would you like that?"

Tiny's eyes widened with excitement. He went back out to the track area to tell his father, when he noticed his dad struggling with the sooty subway cars' couplings cut-lever.

"Can I help you, Dad? Mr. Collins will be a few minutes."

Franklin had already started pulling the cut lever that raised the pin up freeing the connected pair of couplers, but it was stuck. Besides the equipment being rusty and matted with dirt and dust, the trains were pushed too close together. The force of the two heavy subway cars pushed together so tightly made it nearly impossible for the connecting pin to be extracted.

"Dad, do you want me to tell Mr. Collins to finish eating later and move these cars apart a bit and give you some slack?"

Franklin looked at his boy admiringly, knowing he understood the problem. "No, thank you, son. Hand me my halogen tool from the sleeve on my tool bag."

Tiny slid the large crowbar-style bar from the bag and handed it to his father. Tiny knew this tool had several special features that could help his father raise the stuck coupler pin.

Franklin worked up a sweat while unsuccessfully wrestling with the uncoupling, and it ran into his eyes. Rather than wiping his eyes, he placed the halogen bar between the tight couplings and pulled up on the cut lever while leaning his entire body weight onto the halogen tool.

The pin released and the separation was completed, but there was too much built-up pressure in the car-to-car air hose. The hose automatically released upon car-to-car separation and flew about erratically as the air pressure was released.

Like a slow-motion movie, Tiny watched as the propelled air hose struck his father off balance, in the face. Franklin fell backward awkwardly, and his head and halogen bar struck the third rail.

In stunned horror, Tiny watched as his father's entire body twitched uncontrollably, and smoke engulfed his head. Like a melting candle, his father's face imploded as the eyes popped out of their sockets and the once-round face became a ghastly, flat piece of smoking flesh.

After several horrifying minutes, Franklin's body convulsed, flew off the third rail and fell, lifeless on the tracks.

Tiny was horrified and tried to make sense out of what had just happened. He had watched his father put too much pressure on the halogen tool, causing him to lose his balance upon separation of the coupling. He also saw the flailing pressurized air hose strike his dad, knocking him further off balance and onto the third rail. In this ancient abandoned railroad line, the wood covering the third rail had either deteriorated or was never there in the first place.

The MTA third rail carried 600 volts, but if a person was wet or sweating, the voltage increased. His sweating father never had a chance. Franklin's pride had probably prevented him from asking his son or Mr. Collins to help him.

Mr. Collins saw the end of the tragedy and became unglued.

He ran in a circle then stopped and looked again. Then he ran into the rest shack, then back out again.

A knowing calm came over Tiny as he steadily picked up his father's large key ring and bag of tools. He backtracked his way to his father's locker and removed all the keys and items that he thought could come in handy.

Tiny was aware of all the train schedules and tracks, so he coolly walked to the platform that would take him home. He did not know how to drive, so his father's car sat in Hudson Yards as Tiny rode the train home.

"**A**re you sure he won't be home soon?" an anxious Walter asked.

"Don't be silly. He'll probably even work overtime again. This is the time of year when the railways are the busiest. Silly union rules require that each worker must perform their personal job title duties, no matter how easy they are. An engineer cannot do a brakeman's job and so on. They won't be back for hours." She grinned.

Walter was the Wilson's next-door neighbor. He was much younger than Franklin, but still feared him. Walter enjoyed the mature enthusiasm of Dee as their adulterous affair continued. He was a lazy goof-off who lived at home with his parents and mooched off them.

The pair were naked under the sheets when Walter said, "I have an early Christmas present for you."

"You just gave me one silly," she cooed.

Walter stood up and pulled a small gift-wrapped box from his trousers lying on the floor.

Grinning from ear to ear, he silently handed her the present.

Dee eagerly removed the long red ribbon and peered into the box. A simple red scarf perched neatly on a bed of cotton. Knowing her paramour was unemployed, she feigned surprise and excitement over the gift.

"You shouldn't have. The ribbon is lovely, and look . . . a red scarf came with the pretty box," she said.

They hugged and became passionate again when Dee said, "Wrap the scarf on my neck, Walter. I want to make love again with my gift proudly displayed."

The amorous pair climbed out of bed and stood in front of a desktop mirror as Walter seductively placed the red scarf around her swan-like neck. That's when they both saw Tiny standing in the doorway.

Without a word, Tiny strangled Walter right after he snapped his mother's dainty neck. Tiny was surprised at his composure as he packed a suitcase with things he needed.

Tiny calmly made himself a huge meal of leftover chicken, mashed potatoes, and collard greens. Then he traveled by rail back to Penn Station and disappeared into the nether-world below.

CHAPTER

2

"**M**icko! Chief Clifford wants you down at the puzzle palace pronto!" Detective Sergeant Duffy bellowed.

Micko looked up from his computer in surprise, and before he could say a word, Duffy yelled, "Lopez! You drive him there now!"

Duffy rushed back into his office with a bang as he slammed the door shut.

"What was that all about?" Gus Lopez asked Micko.

"I don't know. This is a mystery to me."

Detective Gus Lopez and Detective Mick O'Shaughnessy had been partners for years. On rare occasions, Micko was given special assignments because he had an unusual flair for successfully completing them.

Micko nodded to Gus, then toward Sgt. Duffy's office, and they simultaneously walked to see their boss. Duffy was angrily pushing papers around when Micko gently knocked on the door.

Duffy looked up, then irritably waved them in.

"What's up with you, O'Shaughnessy? Are you banging the chief's daughter or something?" he asked.

"No, boss, I have no idea what this is about."

"I don't like getting calls from the Chief of Detectives demanding an audience with one of my detectives." He scowled.

"Trust me, Sarge, I don't like it either."

"What's this about you working a case in Penn Station a few years back?"

"That was a long time ago. There was a character pointlessly shooting commuters with a .25 caliber revolver during the morning rush hour. A task force was set up between the NYPD and the then Penn Station police officers. Three random people were wounded, and then it just stopped. Some figured that the gunman, or woman, felt pressure from the task force and quit. I thought that two of the shootings were random to disguise the real target. Others felt that the shooter either died, got arrested and went to prison on an unrelated charge, or was in the military and was deployed overseas. In any event, the shootings stopped, and the case remains open."

"Well, apparently your expertise in not solving that case just got you assigned to another in Penn Station," Duffy growled sarcastically.

Gus tried to hide a snicker, but Duffy caught him.

"Don't think you're getting assigned to this, Lopez. You will now catch both your cases and O'Shaughnessy's," he said.

The two detectives left the 52nd Precinct Detective Squad supervisor's office with more questions than when they entered. Gus grabbed the keys to the unmarked car and they went to police headquarters in lower Manhattan.

On the ride Gus asked Micko, "So what was that .25 caliber shooting all about?"

"It was like I said to Duffy. Three nonfatal shootings had the Penn Station commuters in an uproar. I'm not sure whose idea it was for the task force, but I got assigned. The railroad police thought we were interfering and we thought they should've handled it on their own, so we didn't get along."

"So who got shot and why?" Gus persisted.

"Two men and a woman. Apparently the shooter walked along the Penn Station Concourse during the morning rush hour with thousands of other commuters racing to connecting trains or exits. While in a thick group of people, the shooter stuck the gun into the victim's back and fired. The blast was muffled by the close contact and the noisy rushing of travelers. By the time the victim fell to the ground and passersby even noticed, the shooter was long gone. It just seemed like random targets. End of story."

Before long, the Bronx detectives were at 1 Police Plaza announcing themselves to the burly officer guarding the entrance to Chief Clifford's office.

They were quickly ushered into the lavish office of the NYPD Chief of Detectives.

"It's nice to see you again, detectives," Chief Clifford said warmly as he shook their hands. Have a seat. Do you wish for some coffee or other refreshment?" he asked.

"No, thanks," they both answered in unison.

"Well, let me get right down to it. There has been the usual string of missing persons reported during this holiday season, but two missing women do not fit the pattern, and the only common denominator is that they went missing in the very early morning hours while waiting for trains departing from Penn Station."

Chief Clifford paused for effect as the seriousness of the situation sank into the minds of the two detectives.

"It appears that we may have a serial kidnapper lurking in the depths of Penn Station's underground caverns. Since there are no ransom requests, we have to assume the worst. If this is so, then we have a serial killer on our hands. I don't need to tell you what will happen if the news media confirms this, so we are putting together an NYPD, Amtrak PD, and FBI task force. Last year a particularly obnoxious reporter ran a series of articles about the Phantom of Penn Station who allegedly abducted people. We ran counter articles explaining that the missings were runaways, thrill seekers, and addicts. This time we have missing persons that do not fit that mold."

The chief studied each detective closely before he continued. "O'Shaughnessy, you have worked in this station before I was chief so I need you as the NYPD member on this task force because of your experience. Lopez, wait outside."

Gus reluctantly rose and walked outside the chief's office into the waiting room.

"Micko, I need your help desperately on this one. If these vanishings continue, my tenure as Chief of Detectives is over. We worked as a great team during that Hart Island fiasco, so I'm teaming up with you again. Please don't let me down."

Chief Clifford liked Detective O'Shaughnessy's gritty street smarts and "take no prisoners" attitude. His work on other high-profile cases abroad brought numerous accolades for himself and the NYPD. Since Micko had some knowledge of the vast intertwined chaos known as the world of the railroads underground tunnel system, he was an obvious choice to partake in the task force.

"I will do my best, but I don't work well with other members of task forces and other departments. Too much rivalry, jealousies, and testosterone. No one shares information, so it's like working the case as a blind man."

"I know, Micko, I know. Just give it a shot and if you need to work in an unconventional way, talk to me."

For the next two hours, Micko and the chief perused all the current information on the case. One female was in Manhattan shopping after work and the other commuted in to do some holiday shopping and sightseeing. The victims purchased a ticket to ride a train back to the suburbs and apparently waited alone on a platform and were never seen again.

Micko complained to the chief that many people go missing at Christmas time for a wide variety of reasons, and this task force might be a knee-jerk reaction. The chief was adamant about creating the task force to cover his ass just in case there was foul play involved, and the Phantom of Penn Station articles re-appeared.

The victims varied in age, size, and race. There was no connection to their home residence or other family members. Like the .25 caliber shooter, these women seemed to be random targets waiting on empty platforms between 11:00 p.m. and 1:00 a.m.

Micko read everything with growing frustration, but something bugged him. He pushed away the missing persons' reports and walked across the spacious office to the floor-to-ceiling windows that looked down on the hostile city.

"What do you see? Any connection between the victims?" the anxious chief asked.

"I'm not sure," Micko replied slowly, as he walked about the room. It was a couple of weeks before Christmas, and he noted the chief already had numerous Christmas cards pinned against one wall and nearly a dozen poinsettia adorned the office.

Suddenly it hit him. Red! The two victims were dressed in red. The pair of sleuths compared the victims' clothing descriptions and they both wore holiday red coats, hats, gloves, and scarves. Of course many women wore red at this time of year, but it was a start.

"Chief, you don't need a task force of detectives, you need a flood of uniformed officers to man the platforms and escort women dressed in red. There is no proof that a madman is hiding in the bowels of the vast underground system. If we find proof, then we just need to flush him out with a decoy policewoman dressed in red. She can wait on a seemingly unoccupied platform with her backup team in hiding."

Chief Clifford was ecstatic. He now had a purpose and a plan to set things into motion that would make him look like a genius. He knew that even the best minds sometimes cannot see the obvious, but a fresh set of eyes can often pick up a clue that others overlook.

"Micko, you are a detective prodigy, and I am going to buy you dinner!" he said.

Micko thought fast and replied, "Great, Chief. Gus and I will meet you around the corner in Darby's Steakhouse."

CHAPTER

3

Tiny enjoyed his newfound freedom in his netherworld. His father had taught him well. Tiny had keys to most active and long abandoned train stations. He had keys not just for the MTA but also for secret locations for the Amtrak tunnels, the Long Island Railroad, and the NJ Transit System.

Franklin Wilson made a copy of all these locations with maps included. It was not a well-known fact that rival brakemen sometimes would contract work to other brakemen for a fee. If an Amtrak brakeman was called into work on his day off to perform a needy train coupling, he was paid a full day's pay for a single job. If the Amtrak worker couldn't come in, he would call another brakeman from another railroad to do the job. The replacement would be provided a nice fee for covering the assigned brakeman, who was rewarded with some nice overtime pay.

This trust made everybody richer and bosses didn't care as long as the necessary job got done right. Franklin's maps were the envy of employees that had more seniority because no one knew all the tunnels and abandoned tracks, caverns, stations, passageways, and hidden rooms. Even Franklin did not know all, but Tiny vowed to be the Daniel Boone of the underworld.

He knew most of the places on his father's maps, since his dad had been bringing him to work for the past ten years. He knew the law would be looking for him, and he also knew they would never find him down here. His father taught him about all the dangers of the lower levels including the third rail and crossover rail switches that could catch your foot in the way of an oncoming train. He was also aware of the dangerous homeless. Some were hopeless Vietnam vets, refugees, drug addicts, antisocial loons, criminals on the run, gang members selling drugs or looting the helpless, and runaways. The vast city beneath the city could be more dangerous than topside.

Tiny needed to set up residence far away from the maddening underground crowd. His father had a secret place where they had spent time during his shifts. When he was at work and did simple track changes or couplings, Franklin had to be onsite for the full day and await new work orders. With his job done, Franklin and Tiny had explored this cavernous underground world.

Tiny dragged his suitcase and large tool bag directly to the secret place. Luckily he was a big, strong, young man. When he reached the clandestine site, he pulled out his father's key chain and slowly looked for the correct key.

In moments, he had the massive, filthy, brass door opened and he stepped inside a huge vestibule with tall cathedral ceilings. Incredibly, there was still electricity and most of the interior lights worked. The gigantic hall was the remnants of an abandoned fine restaurant while another equally huge structure was built upon it many years ago.

Franklin liked this place because he knew the fabled history of the bistro, and the unusual cleanliness of the long, deserted rooms. Like hundreds of underground facilities, running hot and cold water, electricity, and steam heat were still present.

His father had told him, "Son, this place was called the Calabrese Bistro back in the day. It was owned by a famous mobster and was a popular hangout for celebrities and racketeers. The art deco that adorns the dining area was very trendy at that time. Unfortunately, the owner was found floating in the East River one bright Sunday morning. He was allegedly knocked off by a rival gangster faction. The bistro had a back-tax problem, so Uncle Sam had it shut down. Many years later as Penn Station underwent major renovations, other cafés were built on top of this once famous bistro."

Today, Tiny looked fondly up at the sign his father had made for him that read, Tiny's Place. Many of the amenities were missing but enough remained, plenty for one man.

The uninhibited bistro was relatively sanitary. The high cathedral ceilings sported numerous gothic paintings and tall Roman pillars surrounded the ornate dining hall.

The enormous kitchen had a rear room for servant quarters, complete with beds and a working bathroom with a single-stall shower. Tiny knew he could live comfortably there. He put his bags down, fell onto a bed, and cried deeply for the loss of his father. Although exhausted from the day's turbulent events and the long weeping session, he jumped out of bed with a start.

The front door! Did I lock it?

He ran to the colossal brass door and realized he had not taken the rusty padlock from the outer door and placed it on the clasp on the inside door. His father had installed a thick 9-inch solid brass lock and door reinforcer on the inside door to keep out vagrants. Although this entrance was hidden in the rear of a garbage-packed alley, Tiny was fearful of discovery by scavengers.

Once Tiny secured the door, he once again felt safe. Now he could do a detailed exploration of Tiny's Place. He was pleased with his new home. Being antisocial, he knew he could easily amuse himself sightseeing and discovering other hidden treasures like his new home. His father had only exposed him to a small portion of the underground kingdom that he was now free to roam.

The first few days spent in Tiny's Place were exciting for Tiny, but he had recurring nightmares, not of his father's death, but of the red scarf around his mother's neck.

Tiny wrestled with options to clear his head of these unsettling visions. He could not have nightmares every night, so he went for long walks late at night. He knew Amtrak crews unloaded the dining coaches and restocked them with fresh sandwiches every night. The day-old food was left in a large hamper to be wheeled out to the loading dock when the garbage truck arrived.

Franklin had shown him how to grab a sandwich or two before they were disposed of. Since each hoagie was tightly wrapped, they were still curiously fresh at the end of the day.

With his father, Tiny often snuck into the dining car area through metal gratings beneath active train platforms. They would carefully slink along the tunnel walls so commuters waiting for their train could not see them. This was how Tiny fed himself those first daunting nights.

Still, he had sleepless nights, haunted by the red scarf and his dead mother.

One night as he approached a narrow passage adjacent to a lower Amtrak platform, he glimpsed a lone commuter waiting for her train. The woman wore a red coat, thigh-high black leather boots, and a red scarf with a snowman printed on it. Red scarf flashed in his mind. Suddenly, he knew how to end his nightmares.

He quietly sneaked up behind the unsuspecting woman and snapped her neck as easily as breaking a pretzel. He quickly threw the body over his shoulder and moved silently into the shadows of the passageway he had come from.

Tiny acted on wild instinct, as he hid the body in a light-less hallway. He slipped through deserted alleys and corridors until he reached the Amtrak coach dining car depot. The work crew used large plastic cargo bins to offload refuse and restock afterward. Tiny stole one while nobody watched.

Before long, Tiny had the woman's body cradled in the push-cart as he returned to Tiny's Place. He was exhausted. Murdering a woman and bringing her body back to his home was the last thing he was thinking of, but it happened. Tiny enjoyed a rare feeling of accomplishment. Murder was quite a rush for him.

Tiny used elaborate routes whenever he left his shelter. He did not want to be seen by any of the Mole People, so he climbed though remote grates, unused, rusty stairwells, and rat-infested sewer systems. When bringing this corpse back to his lair, he had to often carry both body and cart on his back as he trekked through dangerous terrain.

The cadaver was placed in the huge, walk-in refrigerator located in the basement of his refuge. Incredibly, the fridge-freezer still worked. It was completely empty except for a few livestock hooks dangling from an overhead rail. Tiny hung his victim by her coat onto a hook and watched as her lifeless body hung limp. He knotted the red scarf tightly around the cadaver's neck.

The bad dreams stopped for several days but eventually returned with a vengeance. In his new dreams, Tiny was being chased around his new home by the ghostly image of his naked, dead mother with the red scarf flailing as she hounded him.

"We can't do this," Gus cried.

"Sure we can," Micko grinned. "I just helped the chief get a step up on his investigation, so we earned this free meal."

"Was this place *his* suggestion or yours, bucko?" Gus said.

"Hey, pal, we are in Manhattan and we are going to eat the best Manhattan steaks before we go back to da Bronx," Micko joked back.

The pair of detectives were seated at the chief's private table, nursing drinks while they waited on their boss. When he strode toward their table with his head held up high, he beamed with self-confidence.

"Detectives, your timely insight on this case has just put a feather in my cap," he said. Chief Clifford was immediately approached by an eager waiter who was wary of the two men seated at his personal table.

"Get you anything, sir?"

"Yes, Andre, scotch on the rocks, and make that a double."

"So, Chief, now that you have a handle on this case you

probably don't need me or Gus to be assigned to your task force," Micko said.

"No, no, *you* are going to be an integral part of my team. Gus, you can resume your duties at the 52 squad."

Micko saw the disappointment in Gus's face and quickly yelled, "Andre! Another pint of Guinness for me and another sangria for my partner."

Both Gus and the chief shot a knowing wink at Micko.

When the drinks were received and the meal order given, the chief asked Micko, "What is the first thing you are going to do involving this case?"

Micko had a pensive look on his face for a few moments and slowly answered, "I would do a citywide detective squad canvass to see if anybody has a recent open homicide where red clothing was involved. Then I would contact the FBI and see if their VICAP system has a similar MO."

Chief Clifford smiled broadly at Micko's answer. He knew that the FBI's Violent Criminal Apprehension Program (VICAP) was the best place to search for similar modus operandi (MO).

"Those were the calls I just made that caused my delay getting here," he said. "Plus, I'm looking into your idea of an undercover female red riding hood."

"Ok, then, I would seek out the senior Amtrak police officer and find out all I could about the Mole People and the numerous hiding spots underground between here and Grand Central Station. You know, Chief, this prick could be following these women on the train and abducting them well out of our jurisdiction. In fact, they just might be normal missing persons and there isn't any kidnapper."

Gus furtively sipped on his sangria as the others engaged

in a conversation he was not privy to. This back and forth continued throughout dinner. Eventually the chief shook each detective's hand and bade them farewell.

"I'm glad that's over," Gus slurred as he threw the car keys to Micko.

"Too much sangria?" Micko asked.

"Too much sangria," Gus answered.

CHAPTER

4

Tiny was very concerned about the elusive routes he took from his dwelling while doing routine things. Finding food was easy, cleaning his clothes at 4:00 a.m. in the all-night laundromat was easy, and buying small household items was easy. This was, after all, New York City—the city that never sleeps. Convenience stores, pizza parlors, and other eateries were open late. There were numerous street-level panhandlers that paid Tiny for protection, so money was never a problem.

His dilemma was leaving and returning to his home simply, yet secretly. After studying his father's maps, Tiny drew his own maps, which included evasive routes and flat ground where the pushcart would be most effective.

Even though Tiny was considered a simple person with an underdeveloped mind, his mind flourished in other ways. He was a virtuoso when it came to reading, retracing, or drawing maps. He was able to configure several maps that would allow him to see clear paths wherever he wished to go.

Living in a primeval setting would drive most people mad, but Tiny relished the daily struggle to subsist. His primitive instincts fueled by the will to survive helped him overcome these obstacles. Soon, Tiny had a map system that made his father's obsolete.

But, still, there were the recurring hallucinations that abated after each murder. He now had two dead, red-clothed women hanging in the meat locker, yet the nightmares continued.

He found that by tying red scarves around the cadavers' necks, the dreams went away for a longer period of time. Since it was the Christmas season, red scarves were everywhere.

He went back upstairs and wrestled down one of the extra beds from the servants' quarters, then went back for a small dining room table and four chairs. He had the huge refrigerator turned into a mini café with red-scarfed bodies lounging at the table.

Tiny looked admiringly at his bizarre setting for a long time. He hoped the image would burn into his mind and replace the damn pictures of his mother in his dreams.

After Micko dropped Gus off at the precinct, he drove his car to The Wicked Wolf Restaurant to meet his girlfriend, Esmeralda, for a nighttime drink. She was already seated at a quaint little table in a corner with a window view.

"Well, my dear, I have a new work assignment," he proudly said.

After ordering a round of drinks, Micko explained the day's events to his gal pal.

"I bet you could use my help on this case, big boy," she said.

"I sure can, babe. I need you to research all you can on the history of Penn Station, Mole People, and schematics of hidden tunnels and buildings under Penn Station. Then you can text the info to me on my cell phone."

"Sometimes I think you are dating me just because I am a librarian," she said, pretending to be irritated.

"No, I date you because of that incredible body and your invigorating sexual appetite. Besides you're not just a librarian, you are *the* librarian."

They both smiled at each other, the way lovers do, hands touching ever so lightly, giving each other sensual strokes.

"How long do you think this assignment will last?" she asked.

"I don't know. I'm not even sure that there is a case, but if there is one, hopefully our undercover policewoman can lure this bastard into the open for a quick arrest."

"Darling, all this police talk is giving me all kinds of ideas for role-playing tonight," she said.

"I guess we'll skip dessert here and have it in bed," he returned with a provocative smile.

When their drinks were finished, Micko followed Esmeralda to her City Island home, knowing she would get him the best research on his new assignment as well as earth-shattering sex.

The nightmares ceased. Tiny was ecstatic. Now he could concentrate on improving his quality of life in the depths of New York City's underworld. Using his sheer size as a weapon, Tiny acquired many useful comfort items for his shelter. He had a slightly cracked but workable CD player. Next came a very used portable DVD player. Tiny enjoyed action movies and cartoons.

With these new comforts, he expanded his underground horizons. He was the subterranean Daniel Boone, exploring obscure tunnels that twisted and turned throughout his concealed wilderness. He located new and strange places not seen in generations. He yearned to find other clean living quarters scattered about his realm. He needed to conquer the cavernous world he lived in but was troubled by senseless fears.

Living in the dark world caused paranoia to set in. Although his eyes were getting accustomed to the darkness, he quickly lost his night vision when he entered his well-lit abode.

He lowered his lights, listening to music and watching cartoons in total darkness. He prowled his pitch-black kingdom with the help of a pen light. His night vision became sharp, but the paranoia was sharper.

Tiny feared the Mole People, mostly because he had never seen them. His fear of the unknown was a childlike fear. He had heard rumors about the Mole People feasting on rats and humans that dared to enter their lair.

Booby traps! I need booby traps to protect my hideaway, he thought.

He surrounded access points to Tiny's Place with broken bottles. Only he knew how to avoid the sharp shards of glass. He removed dozens of light bulbs that dimly lit the corridors leading from his den to the railroad tunnels. He stacked these bulbs in a crate he kept in his home for future use.

When his paranoia subsided and he felt safe, he resumed doing the things he enjoyed. Hiking, exploring, eating, and peeking in on his red-scarfed ladies. One pretty young white lady and one fat Latina completed his corpse chorus. In his deranged mind, he often brought music and sang with the dead or showed them his DVD cartoons. In his disturbed mind, he wanted more women in his freezer room to keep him company. He was getting bored with the dead duo. He needed the rush a fresh murder would give him.

CHAPTER
5

It was early—very early—and cold when Micko drove down West Side Highway after leaving Esmeralda's house. He wanted to get a feel for Penn Station at 4:00 a.m. Chief Clifford thought he had intimate knowledge of the subterranean world under Penn Station but he was wrong. Although he grew up in a monstrous housing complex and learned the vast interconnecting underground hallways, this would be different.

It was 3:30 a.m. when he pulled into a parking space next to the NYPD Midtown South Precinct at 35th Street between Eighth and Ninth Avenues. He placed his official NYPD parking placard on the dashboard and quickly walked the couple of blocks to Penn Station and entered from the 35th Street entrance. Three bums slept in the vestibule, while two hookers shared a cigarette. This entrance was filthy with empty beer cans and other trash strewn about.

The station had changed dramatically since he was last there. Gone were the rows upon rows of benches that commuters rested on in the waiting room of the huge concourse area. Removed probably because derelicts had taken up residence on the benches on cold days.

The concourse was surrounded by a plethora of shops that made the train station look like a shopping mall. At this hour, trains were not running, so there should be a lack of commuters in the waiting area. He was right. It was like a ghost town.

Micko walked the perimeter of the interior of the station looking between shops and alleys and witnessed numerous unfortunates sleeping under newspapers and dirty blankets. They were homeless and keeping out of sight. The stench of urine was overpowering, and it was in every cubbyhole leading from the main concourse area.

These alleys, out of sight from the public, were crammed with shopping carts, boxes, and transportable living items the bag people carried.

An Amtrak police officer drove by on a small yellow golf cart-type vehicle with police markings. Micko waved him over and identified himself.

"Nice patrol car you have, Officer Gerrish," Micko said, after reading the officer's name tag.

"Hey, it sure beats walking. This little cart can get me into places where bigger vehicles can't. There is so much ground space around here, I can cover it all several times a night, while foot patrol can only do it once."

"I see you still have a homeless problem here. I stepped over three drunks sleeping inside the 35th Street entrance, and I've spotted many more in every cubbyhole around here," Micko said.

"It's a very confusing situation. Commuters and shop owners continuously complain about the homeless, but we are almost helpless in moving them. The current mayor has eased enforcement on quality-of-life crimes, such as public urination, panhandling, sleeping in public, etc. Even though Penn Station is privately owned, a federal judge issued an injunction against the Amtrak Police from ejecting the homeless from our train stations. We have a basic agreement with many of these people to stay out of sight and we will not interfere with them." Officer Gerrish continued. "The bigger problem is the drug addict squatters that take up residency under the train platforms. They get high and build small fires, then nod out. Sometimes *they* go up in flames and sometimes the tracks catch fire. Luckily, there is a group of underground dwellers who scare and chase away the druggies. Fires and police action are bad for their lifestyle and community."

Micko was blown away by this information. He thought the police ejected the homeless each night, and public advocacy groups picked them up and took them to shelters.

Officer Gerrish told Micko there were four other foot officers patrolling the station, and he had to resume his duty.

Micko continued his journey of the main concourse area when heard a voice.

"Hey, detective. What are you doing back here?"

A surprised Micko looked in the direction of the voice and recognized the man walking down the stairs from the 35th Street entrance. He was in his late 60s, small, and walked with a pronounced limp. He was obviously one of the unfortunates that made this train station their return to the womb. Unlike the filthy despots sleeping in the urine-stained alleys, this man's unkempt clothing was clean. An aged U.S. Army fatigue jacket complete with military markings hung off his narrow frame.

"Hello, Joseph, you are looking well."

"How about buying an old pal a cup of java, Micko?"

"What the hell is open at this hour?" Micko laughed.

"Come with me, my uninformed friend, and see what the night people know," he said.

The two men shook hands and did a male hug. Micko remembered when he had worked the .25 caliber shooter case, he observed two husky railroad cops roughing up the cripple. Micko stepped in and used some tough Bronx language to rip the cops a new asshole, thus cementing a friendship with Joe Lombardi.

Joe led Micko a few blocks south from Penn Station to a dingy Chinese restaurant. The place was a beehive of activity. Hookers, pimps, spaced-out druggies, drunks, and wide-eyed tourists filled the booths and tables.

"Mr. Waffles meet Micko." Joe made the introduction.

Mr. Waffles, a huge Chinese man, had a strange resemblance to Oddjob from the movie *Goldfinger*.

"Why do they call him Mr. Waffles?" Micko asked.

"Because he makes breakfast waffles every morning and they are as big as a sewer cover," Joe laughed.

Joe used a distinct type of sign language, and Mr. Waffles brought two coffees with the fixings to their table. The two prepared their coffees in the comfortable silence that only friends can enjoy. Then after a long sip, Micko stated, "This is terrible shit!"

They both laughed as Joe said, "Yeah, but it's the only shit you will get at this hour. Heck its warm and Mr. Waffles keeps us protected."

Then Micko got serious. "Do they still call you The Gimp?"

"Yeah, but after all these years I've accepted it. Besides, I am a gimp," he said.

Micko liked this poor, long-haired hippie, and remembered most of their conversations. Joe Lombardi was drafted near the end of the Vietnam War. He was engaged to his high school sweetheart and expected to marry her after his two-year stint in the U.S. Army was over.

Joe spent a thirteen-month tour of duty in Vietnam and received a Dear John letter from his fiancée. Not only was she leaving him for another man, but the other man was his best friend who had beat the draft by college deferment.

He immediately reenlisted and served another tour of duty as a tunnel rat. Being a small, slightly built man, he was perfect for the job.

In the years prior to the war, the Viet Cong built numerous elaborate underground tunnel systems throughout the countryside. The tunnels were their city, their territory. There were huge underground storage facilities, training and living quarters, and hospitals. Soldiers could stay underground for months at a time.

Whenever the U.S. Army discovered one of these tunnels, the tunnel rats were called in. Armed with a .45 caliber pistol, knife, and flashlight, a tunnel rat would enter the tunnel and kill those inside. If the occupants retreated deeper into the cave system, explosives would be used to kill and destroy the lairs.

The enemy used many methods to defend their hideouts from tunnel rats. Booby traps were placed inside the tunnel entrance, as well as poisonous snakes and scorpions. Small coves next to the entrance contained lookouts armed with spears to stab a tunnel rat entering the lair.

Being a tunnel rat was not for the faint-hearted. It was extremely dangerous as well as tight and claustrophobic. A despondent Joe Lombardi had volunteered for the job and was severely wounded when a booby trap ripped a hole in his pelvis. He was awarded a bronze star, a bevy of other medals, and a permanent limp.

Micko recalled how his pal told him that he now only felt at home in the labyrinths under Penn Station and Grand Central. These tunnels reminded him of the ones in Vietnam. Joe suffered from PTSD that caused severe mood swings and bouts of aggressive and antisocial behavior.

Micko and Joe talked for a while about their lives since they last shared a cup of coffee. Joe was genuinely interested about Micko's overseas adventures as well as the recent arrests for the murders on Hart Island.

The detective learned Joe had finally agreed to speak with an outreach counselor and now lived in a pretty decent single room occupancy with other veterans.

"SRO has its limitations, but it also has a shower," Joe explained. He still sought refuge and comfort in the pits of Penn Station but had a clean, warm place when he needed it.

"Joe, I need your help."

Micko explained his assignment to Joe and his buddy listened intently. The detective asked his friend for any advice about the Mole People.

"It would take a long dinner to catch you up to speed on the underground communities," he answered.

After a sip of coffee, Joe continued. "Remember Sgt. Pedone?"

"Sure I do. He was about the only guy I got along with the last time I worked here."

"Well, now he's a captain. On my good mood days, I sometimes have coffee with him. He was asking me about a new Mole Person who may have killed his own mother. You should talk to Rich Pedone and start growing a scruffy beard. You need to meet the Mole People, but you have to look like one. Then I will show you what I know about the underground life in Penn Station and the underground secret societies."

The pair enjoyed more easy conversation before they parted, knowing they would be seeing each other often during Micko's assignment.

"Well look who's a captain," Micko said as he walked into the Amtrak Police office of Captain Richard Pedone.

"Good Lordy, look what the cat dragged in," the captain said.

The two gave each other a hearty handshake and reminisced about their past interactions. Then they got serious.

"Micko, these Amtrak guys will not be easy to work with. They consider you an interloper, interfering with their investigation. They consider this to be a simple case of missing persons. We get half a dozen each month, especially this time of year. Emotions run high and romances die, too many Christmas parties, renewed feelings of freedom and liberation. You name it, there are hundreds of reasons why people disappear . . . on purpose."

Before Micko could respond he continued. "The FBI guys agreed and took our detectives out for a holiday dinner. There is absolutely no evidence that we have a serial killer hiding in the pits of this station. One of the newspapers is running an old story about a Phantom of Penn Station. This phantom talk is being taken as a joke. There isn't even a body, so you will be virtually working this theory on your own."

Micko thought about this as he slowly walked around the office. Captain Pedone was right, as far as he was concerned. So was Chief Clifford. Micko was caught in the middle.

"Rich, what do you have on a kid who killed his mom and might be hiding below?"

"Oh, the Yonkers cops have that case. It's really a shame. Poor brakeman accidentally gets killed and his backward son witnesses it. The distraught kid races home to tell his mother and he finds her in bed with their neighbor's son. He kills them both and disappears. Yonkers detectives came around here because his dad worked for the MTA for years. We asked around, but no one has seen this kid. His name is Tobias Wilson. I'll pull the file for you."

Micko thanked the captain and explained he would work undercover in the caverns below until his chief pulled him from this assignment.

Captain Pedone looked Micko straight in the eyes for thirty seconds before he said, "I have keys you will need and a pad in the Pennsylvania Hotel that is set aside for us in an emergency."

Ten minutes later, Captain Pedone handed Micko a flashlight for a quick tour of the underground. The Amtrak PD station was one level below the Penn Station main concourse area and was accessed by a steep flight of stairs. From this area, Captain Pedone led Micko along a well-lit passageway to the Amtrak commuter train platforms.

The two walked along the first platform until they reached the end of the podium at track level. They climbed down a short metal ladder to trackside, then went under the platform.

Micko was amazed at the amount of trash entrenched in this area. Empty water and booze bottles, used sets of hypo needles, and fast-food wrappings littered the entire floor space.

"This is where the druggies hang out," Captain Pedone said as he pointed to the trash.

Pedone gave Micko a tour of several platforms and the results were always the same—filthy remains of addicts conducting their nefarious business.

Their next stop was two floors below the platforms, where Micko was led to a large maintenance room. The room was unlocked and packed with huge, dirty machineries. Pedone led the way to the rear of this room where he produced a set of keys and opened a door that led to a small hidden elevator.

Micko always carried his notepad and recorded all he was told and shown. The captain was very organized and each key was labeled. Micko was taken down the elevator to several levels below the commuter train tracks where an older train depot existed. It looked very similar to today's railroad tracks that weaved in and out of Penn Station, only it was never used.

"Why is there still electricity here if it's abandoned?" Micko asked.

"When each new level is built upon the existing level, the power, sewerage, gas, cable, and water lines are used during construction. The sandhogs live below while they are building above. Every few decades, the process continues. Even the lowest level at bedrock has power. People rarely go way down below, but if they need to, power is on."

Micko was amazed at all of the facts Pedone gave him. They walked around what looked like a Currier and Ives painting of a vintage railway terminal, only it was abandoned. Like a scene out of the *Twilight Zone*. No people.

The empty station was decorated with beautiful multicolored-tiled walls, and the platform had ancient trash cans and an old newspaper stand. The entrance had comical wooden turnstiles.

"This is only a few stories below street level, so it still looks nice. It gets a lot spookier the farther down you go," Pedone said.

"How far down does it go?" Micko asked incredulously.

"I've only been down six levels and that was a long time ago," he smiled.

Captain Pedone showed Micko the special, locked entrance to the hotel freight elevator. "As a courtesy, the hotel saves a room for Amtrak officers. In the past, high-ranking officers would use the room while on a layover. Other times, influential guests would be put up here. Then it became abused as officers hosted card games, hookers, and drinking parties. Now I have the key to the room. It hasn't been used in two years. Let's see what it looks like today."

They walked to a side corridor, away from the main platform to what appeared to be a utility room. Again, Captain Pedone produced his key ring.

The rusty lock to the maintenance room creaked loudly as Pedone turned the appropriate key. The room was dirty and damp as their flashlights cut silver beams through the dark. The captain headed for what looked like a badly stained wall but turned out to be the elevator control room.

"Pull this lever down to send power to the elevator," he said.

Seconds after he pulled the lever, the elevator motors whirled and a squeaky mini elevator appeared. Pedone opened the musty old door and they both stepped in. He pressed the up button and away they went.

The elevator stopped at the vestibule in the rear entrance to the Pennsylvania Hotel. It was way off from the hotel's main lobby, but it was clean and uncongested. The secret room door didn't have a number printed on it, but Pedone's key easily opened it.

Micko smiled with delight as he viewed the luxurious room. Obviously, this room was cleaned and maintained just like all the others in the hotel. The foyer was large and painted a soothing, dandelion yellow. The sitting room was similarly painted with pastel-colored furniture, a large television, and a dorm-style refrigerator.

"I'm going to like this," Micko said.

"A word of advice. If you are going to infiltrate the Mole People, you had better only come here when you need a good bath or a clean bed. Do not wash with a fragrance soap or shampoo. I'll have the staff remove those and replace with plain ivory soap," Pedone stated.

Micko finally realized he would have to maintain a completely different mindset as he went undercover, underground.

Am I really cut out for this assignment?

CHAPTER

6

Micko grew a shaggy beard and visited Salvation Army and Goodwill shops in the South Bronx looking for a specific look to fit in with the Mole People. Just as he exited a shop near Fordham Road, he held the door for an elderly Irish woman who struggled with a large suitcase.

"Tanks laddie, oi must dispose av me dear departed 'usband's clothin'."

Suddenly Micko had an idea, so he searched through the woman's suitcase. He took a tattered brown corduroy sports coat and a weathered Irish fisherman's sweater from the bag and gave the grateful woman twenty dollars.

When he returned home, Micko put on his new wardrobe

along with ragged, oil-stained blue jeans that he wore when he rode his motorcycle. He searched through his closet and took out an old Irish cap and his shillelagh. A few more days without shaving would complete his transformation.

Later that night, Micko drove back to Penn Station and met Joe the Gimp who was soliciting from generous Christmastime straphangers.

"So, how do I look?" Micko asked.

"You look like a nutty Irishman," Joe said with a laugh.

The pair discussed Micko's keys to hidden rooms and elevators as well as his new outfit until Joe said, "Let's go to the Papaya King outside. I'm hungry and need some fresh air."

The weather was unusually pleasant for mid-December as the two walked a few blocks until they encountered a filthy, yet attractive homeless woman. She ate a hot dog while two young punks dressed in gothic clothing harassed her.

"Hey bitch, I have a hot dog for you to eat," one punk said, as he grabbed his crotch.

The other punk spit at the woman and laughed loudly at his friend's vulgar demonstration.

Wordlessly, Micko stepped between the waif and her tormentors and struck the laughing hyena in the forehead with his shillelagh and then with an underhand sweep, struck the other in the groin.

They both fell to the ground and like sissies they cried, demanding to know why they were attacked.

"You nu why," is all Micko said, with his best Irish accent.

"Kitty, meet the Nutty Irishman. He helped me out in a similar fashion several years ago," Joe said.

About a dozen homeless persons witnessed this strange act of chivalry and patted Micko on the back. Kitty was very popular among the unfortunates. Most had dogs or cats for pets and Kitty cared for the animals when they were injured or sick. She was also generous when she had extra.

Micko detected a special warmth between Kitty and Joe—the deep look into each other's eyes, the handshake that lingered.

"Nice to meet you, Mr. Nutty Irishman. Thank you. Joe, I must get back and feed my litter," she said, as she briskly walked away.

"Her real name is Doris. She once owned a popular hair salon in the Bronx. Kitty is our version of the cat lady. She cares for close to a dozen of her own and dozens of other people's pets," Joe explained.

"If you wipe off the dirt, she is a remarkably good-looking woman," Micko returned.

Joe smiled slightly and said, "Yes. Yes, she is."

All of this action took place directly in front of the Papaya King kiosk.

"Hey, Hawkeye, how about a couple of franks with the works?" Joe bellowed above the street noise.

"Coming right up, Joe."

"Why Hawkeye?" Micko asked Joe.

"Because he is always out here, on the street, and sees *everything*," Joe said.

In minutes, the hot dogs were ready and Hawkeye said, "These are on me, boys, for taking care of Kitty. You do realize that by now half the underground communities will have heard about this new Nutty Irishman and his Shillelagh Law."

Micko was unwrapping his frankfurter when he heard, "That's him, officer."

An Amtrak police officer stood behind him with the two gothic punks in tow. Before Micko or Joe could say a word, the officer slapped the hot dog out of Micko's grip. Mustard and sauerkraut stuck to the officer's hand and as he slowly wiped his hand on Micko's coat, he leaned over and said, "I don't like you Skells and I don't want you in or around my station. Do I make myself clear?"

"Yes, sir," Micko said.

Joe was rebelliously silent.

"Do I make myself clear?" the officer repeated, directly to Joe.

"Yes, officer, 'e's jist a wee stoned," Micko said.

This appeared to satisfy Johnny Law, as he walked the punks back into the station to catch their rides back to the safety of the suburbs.

"Joe, you have to be more careful. I can't ID myself while I'm going undercover," Micko whispered.

"That's Frank 'Blackjack' Randazzo," Joe muttered. "He hates the homeless and often gets physical and tosses us out of the station on the coldest winter nights."

"Still, you need to be cool with Blackjack and all the Amtrak cops," Micko warned.

Joe knew Micko was right. With a large band of homeless enjoying the great weather and Hawkeye keeping his vigilant watch over his incorrigible flock, Micko's subterfuge would have been blown.

Just then a teenager handed a bag to Joe.

"Hey, Gimp, Hawkeye wrapped these up for you guys. He said it's time you went below," the kid said.

"Thanks, Rooster," Joe said.

The teenager was a black youth with an unusual-shaped afro, where Micko guessed the nickname Rooster came from.

"What's his story?" Micko asked, quizzically.

"He's a runner. He lives aboveground but runs important

errands for the Mole People. Radio is the other runner," Joe said.

"Let's go find a quiet place to eat. I have many questions to ask you, Joe."

Since the main entrance to Penn Station was being watched by Blackjack, Joe decided to take Micko to the lower levels using one of his special access points.

Micko was surprised at how well Joe the Gimp knew the streets and dark alleys and how fast he walked with the limp. Soon they were outside a dreary storefront that read, "West Side Psychic & Tarot Readings."

Joe knocked on the door and an older woman asked, "Who?"

"Ambrosia, it's the Gimp. I'm going to the rear of your shop. Don't let Butch out," he answered.

He led Micko quietly to the rear and opened a small grating that led underground. Joe produced a small but powerful flashlight and silently climbed down the rusty ladder rings.

Micko kept quiet and figured Butch was either a gun-toting resident or a very large dog.

It was a long, dark, weary climb down the ancient ladder. The shaft led to a poorly lit, damp, unused sewer system. The ceiling was only about four feet high, so they walked stooped over. There was also a foot of sewerage flowing on the floor, so the pair had to duck and walk with wide strides to keep their feet dry.

They were silent for several blocks when Micko asked, "What the hell is this?"

"If you live underground, you will travel like this often," Joe said.

He continued. "Always keep your feet dry. No one knows what is in these waters. If you travel a tunnel for the first time, bring chalk. When you come to an intersection, use the chalk and mark arrows to indicate which way you came from. We often find skeletons who lost their way."

Thirty minutes later, the sewer tunnel they were walking through emptied into a large reservoir of putrid seawater. Joe explained this sewer was one of many abandoned, filled with a backflow of water from the Hudson River during high tide. They were deep in the bowels of the underbelly of Manhattan; now they had to climb back up. This far on the west side, everything led to the Hudson River: tunnels, sewers, train tracks, power, steam, and gas lines.

Joe led Micko up a rickety, old, iron stairway to upper levels overlooking the reservoir below. Here stood a dimly lit cavernous room crowded with rusty timeworn machinery.

"Before you ask, I do not know," Joe said.

They walked through the huge room and exited at an old, abandoned railroad station with a string of broken-down freight cars, an engine, and a red caboose.

"This freight line spur ran west from Penn Station and hooked up with the Hudson Freight line service going north and south. It ran parallel to the 34th Street IRT Ninth Avenue line. Both were discontinued in 1940. There are numerous abandoned stations under NYC and most have freight trains or subway cars. I lived in this ancient caboose for many years," Joe said.

He climbed the rear metal stairs to the caboose and opened the creaky tail door. The interior was breathtakingly clean and adorned with antique railroad memorabilia.

"This is fabulous!" Micko exclaimed.

"I've collected mementos from many years of living down here. Even though I have my SRO aboveground, this is my fortress of solitude. Part of my PTSD and previous tunnel rat occupation makes me crave tight, yet comfortable, spaces.

Mentally I guess it's like returning to the womb. On my anti-social days, I come here," he said.

Micko explored the small yet comfortable carriage. A six-foot-long bunk ran along each wall. The top of the bunks opened, revealing storage space under one and a cooler system under the other. One bunk had sleeping supplies neatly folded, along with bathroom provisions and cooking utensils.

The cooler bunk contained the normal family requirements. A small dining room table was fixed in one corner of the stateroom while a small desk was located at the opposite corner next to an ancient potbelly stove. The dining table had a small microwave, hot plate, and a coffee maker that Joe must have added to the vintage wooden carriage.

High above the bunks ran a series of mini ceiling lights and shelves that contained elaborate, antique wood carvings of locomotives, collectible railroad lanterns, and vest watches, along with rare photos.

"How . . . what?" Micko asked.

"Very easy," Joe said. "Under the station platform is the power source. I just ran electric cable and transferred juice to my little coach. There is power everywhere underground. Behind the platform is a nice bathroom with a hot and cold running shower that was used by the sandhogs before the station was closed down."

"This is absolutely amazing, Joe."

"No, what is amazing is that I'm going to let you live here while you are undercover. Just swear to me that you will never divulge the location to anyone," Joe said.

"Done deal!"

The pair sat on opposite bunks facing each other, eating the hot dogs and making small talk as Joe lit up a joint.

"Now tell me about these aboveground runners," Micko said.

"Rooster and Radio are allowed contact with the various Mole People. Some communities allow them entrance while others leave notes in hidden locations. They both have a residence aboveground and the secret societies use their Manhattan address to receive mail and financial benefits. Rooster was once a runner for a Bronx numbers' guy. Rooster saw his boss get whacked by a rival numbers' gangster and went into hiding here. Radio is the information guy. He knows all of the local gossip that the secret societies mayors need to know."

Joe inhaled deeply and held the pot in for several seconds before blowing a plume up toward the ceiling.

"It sounds silly, but life underground has become complicated, yet organized for some. The homeless bag people live at street level. They beg for food money and sleep in alleys and doorways. In the first level under the numerous train platforms, live the junkies. They get high and pass out. This area is called the Eye of the Needle.

"These are the underground squatters that the commuters see most often and complain about. The Amtrak Police round them up frequently and toss them out. The junkies make unattended fires, leave trash behind, and use the area as their personal bathroom. These creeps are temporary visitors who come and go with no respect for the subterranean dwellers."

Joe took another hit on his joint, then continued.

"A few levels lower live Hannity's Rats. He calls his community Hannity's Manor. Hannity is a defrocked criminal lawyer who is borderline insane but keeps his community well organized. Hannity ensures each member of the community applies for welfare, food stamps, or disability. He arranges electronic transfer of payment to the Chase Bank on 34th Street.

With this monthly flow of funds coupled with cash from theft, drug sales, and prostitution, the community thrives. Like a socialist society, the funds are shared among the needy ruled by Hannity."

Micko jumped up and stared at Joe in disbelief.

Joe smirked and continued. "Hannity holds all the ATM cards and their corresponding PIN numbers. He uses the runners to obtain cash and provisions from topside when needed. Everything from fresh food to toiletries. Hannity tries to keep his flock under strict control, but with the underground madness, it's a difficult job."

Joe finished his pot and stood up to reach under his bunk and produce two water bottles. He handed one to Micko and opened the other.

"Hannity doesn't want his residents to look like or act like Skells. It's all right if they are dirty and smell, but there are strict rules about fighting, rape, stealing from others, or getting infested with lice. Once a month, each dweller must take a shower and be checked for lice. There is an abandoned railroad workers bunkroom that has a working shower that Moles must use monthly."

Joe took a long drink from his water bottle then continued. "Hannity's Rats often chase out the junkies from under the platforms to help out the police. Each month the police round up the tenants that have lice and take them to the hospital to be treated and cleaned. This works well for both parties."

Micko learned Hannity would often fly into uncontrollable rages and punish his rats. Public beatings were common in an attempt to discourage violating Hannity's Law.

Each woman living in Hannity's Manor was assigned various jobs: cooking, cleaning, laundry, lice grooming, medical treatment for sickness and injuries, caring for the community's pets, and prostitution. Hannity had a huge underground library and a MASH-style hospital, also run by the women.

The men were also assigned various jobs. The saner men were community police called centurions who were Hannity's eyes and ears in the Manor. Others were raiders who ejected the junkie community from the Eye of the Needle. Then there were the pickpockets and beggars that preyed on the topside commuters. Another group secured free food for the community by grabbing leftovers from the Amtrak coach and dining cars or collecting discarded food from fast food shops. Everyone had a job and Hannity was the lord of the manor.

Joe described the communities in the lower depths, far below Hannity's Rats. These nomads, called Skells, were unsociable misfits suffering a multitude of mental problems. They lived in utter filth, were lice ridden, and grossly underfed. Some were former members of Hannity's Rats who were kicked out for failing to follow Hannity's Laws.

The Skells had a short life expectancy. Without rules or punishment, they killed each other for a slice of bread. Rape was rampant; knife fights were a daily routine. Most Skells lived alone and if one Skell invaded another's territory or hovel, there would be a fight to the death.

Hannity's Raiders often trespassed through Skell territory to dispose of the dead. Armed with great numbers, these enforcers met little resistance as lone Skells hid in fear.

Micko drank from his water bottle and took notes on all the incredible information, while Joe kept talking.

Heading north along the Hudson Yards, living in a huge abandoned cave system, were the Vietnam Vets who called their home The Hanoi Hilton. Although these veterans suffered from egregious mental and physical ailments, they banded together to help each other. The bond of service and battle served as a glue that would stick forever. They might argue daily and be complete opposites, but they were brothers.

Like Hannity's Rats, the vets had similar rules for living in The Hanoi Hilton. Everyone shared, so there was no need to steal. Women lived with the men—consensual sharing. The men from this community had various skills and built fine lodges and a huge entertainment tent complete with television sets and a stereo system. Another tent was set up with a bar and several old couches for lounging while drinking or drugging. Tents were necessary since water seeped down through the high brick dome that covered the settlement.

Far below The Hanoi Hilton, at the bedrock level, was an enormous tunnel system running west from the Hudson River, east to the East River. This was where the Morlocks lived. Morlock Nation, residing underground where the sun never reached and most ancient light bulbs had burned out long ago, was named for the H.G. Wells creatures from the classic, *The Time Machine*.

These people never had contact with the aboveground people. They lived and thrived in this barely inhabitable world, long abandoned by modern man. These tunnels were cut from the bedrock hundreds of years ago. As man built contemporary structures above the existing ones, underground dwellers sought the safety below. Like prehistoric man, these Mole People barely scraped out a living, but still survived and thrived. They were the descendants of the original Mole People two hundred years ago.

Micko waved his hands at Joe and asked, "Are you making this shit up as you go? Are you stoned from one joint?"

Joe smiled as he saw his pal's reaction to his narration.

"You will see much of this on your own while you search for your killer. I'm just giving you a heads up, buddy boy."

Micko sat down and listened and learned more about the underground kingdom. North along the Hudson Freight Line, there was a community of young runaways that lived under Riverside Drive. These runaways came to New York for a variety of reasons: to find fame and fortune; escape a predatory environment at home; seek excitement in The Big Apple; or leave a dull existence. The reasons were endless, but the results were the same: broke, homeless, jobless, hungry, and alone.

Fearing the older homeless communities, the runaways built their own. Being young, they had similar interests and ideas. The community quickly grew, but soon the predators came, with rape and robbery a daily routine. To protect themselves, the runaways extended hospitality to criminals hiding from the law. In exchange, the criminals protected the runaways.

The wanted men would come and go, but New York never had a shortage of criminals. Also, the many graffiti artists used the abandoned tunnels as their canvas and hid in this community.

Ali was the current mayor of the runaway community located deep under the 79th Street Rotunda. There was a secret grating allowing access to the rusty ladder that led from the street to below. Like in other communities, each member of the Rotunda Kids had a job. Some worked in the public showers nearby, others delivered dry cleaning to the Riverside Drive wealthy, and others collected bottles or did odd jobs. Some were able to get public assistance while some had money sent from home. Collectively, they lived fairly well.

The Rotunda Kids lived in a huge horseshoe-shaped cave connected to a seventy-five-foot-wide tunnel that ran from

72nd Street to 123rd Street. Here railroad tracks merged into a gigantic abandoned underground railroad yard. Huge cinder block rooms lined this tunnel and the runaways made their homes here. They ate at local soup kitchens, bathed at the public showers, and did their laundry at twenty-four-hour laundromats.

Ali was a good mayor and kept the Rotunda Kids safe and almost drug-free. That was the rule. No drugs. Period. Get high outside, not inside. They lived in harmony in a part of town that few could afford.

Micko asked, "What about the other direction, going east to Grand Central Station?"

"You mean the Waldorf Astoria Gays? Many years ago a huge train terminal was built under the famous Waldorf Astoria Hotel. This terminal held deadhead trains and was used as a workshop to repair locomotives. There is a thriving community of gay men who moved there to avoid persecution from the other communities. Although all communities are scattered with gays, this community is exclusive."

Micko rolled his eyes and said, "I think I'm overdosing on all of this information."

Joe flashed a smile as he reached into his bunk, and proclaimed, "Here is my personal map of New York's underground cave, train, tunnel, and community system."

CHAPTER

7

Tiny's nightmares continued. He still played games with his victims, spoke to them, and watched DVD movies with them, but it wasn't enough. The dreams persisted.

He knew the police must be looking for him and grabbing a new victim would be extremely dangerous, yet he looked forward to adding another red-scarfed victim to his growing family. He picked up a recently discarded newspaper and read about the police hunting for the Phantom of Penn Station, who might be kidnapping women off train platforms.

Late at night, Tiny haunted train platforms, looking for the right woman. He spotted the extra police presence on all train stages in Penn Station. He sat in a small cul-de-sac next to a noisy transformer room and placed his head in his hands thinking, *A diversion, I need a diversion.*

Tiny devised a plan to locate the woman he wished to kidnap and then go to the opposite platform and cut power to the lights. He hoped the police would leave his intended victim's platform and converge on the darkened platform, giving him a chance to make his move. With excited anticipation, Tiny went back to his home base and had a peaceful sleep.

The next day Tiny prepared for the night's task. He gathered the tools he needed and placed them in his father's work bag. He oiled the wheels on his pushcart for stealth purposes. He was ready.

Tiny worked his way to the train platforms from level-two floors below. He navigated through a series of gloomy steam pipe corridors. Nobody lived there and repairmen rarely came through this dark area. The ground was even and flat, making for an easy travel with the cart.

When Tiny came to a much narrower passageway, he left the cart below a circular stairway rising up to an area just below the Metro North train platforms. He carefully carried his tool bag over his shoulder, like a knapsack, as he climbed the unsteady metal stairway. The stairs led to a large metal door that opened at track level, thirty feet away from the platforms.

Tiny slithered forward along the shadowy tracks toward each platform, one at a time, until he observed a woman dressed in a heavy black leather coat with a bright red scarf around her neck. She waited for the Hudson Line train going to Harrison, New York.

Knowing her train might arrive any minute, Tiny quickly crossed the tracks to the opposite platform taking commuters to Scarsdale, New York. He was far enough down the darkened tracks to avoid prying eyes. After he opened the fuse box, he used a plier tool to damage the fuse illuminating the platform, so waiting passengers couldn't see each other.

Once the platform went dark, a series of cries and alerts of concern were echoed by the commuters waiting for their ride home. Tiny quickly returned to the other platform with the red-scarfed lady. All eyes were on the opposite platform where police rushed with spears of light from cheap flashlights.

Tiny crept onto the rear end of the platform with his intended victim in sight. He stayed in the shadows until he was right behind her. While people looked across the tracks, he quickly snatched the woman from behind and pulled her into the shadows. There he shattered her neck and tossed her lifeless body over his shoulder.

Tiny retreated the way he had come as the uproar on the darkened platform increased. Nobody knew the pretty woman with the red scarf was missing. As big and strong as Tiny was, he had trouble carrying the lady and the tool bag down the wobbly metal stairwell. Once he reached the bottom of the stairs, he placed victim number three into the cargo bin and easily wheeled her to his lair unnoticed.

Back at Tiny's Place, he propped the pretty lady up in a chair at the small card table. He stepped back to observe his new addition to the red-scarf family. She was a light-skinned black woman with small bones, yet a nice figure. She wore her hair in a neat mini afro style and there was a little red ribbon just above her right ear.

Tiny was very pleased with his new acquisition. He immediately talked to her and told her how beautiful she was and how he approved of her hairstyle and choice of clothing, especially the red adornments. He sat with his red-scarfed family for hours, enjoying senseless conversations. The man finally felt at ease and was invigorated by this dangerous killing and kidnapping. The risk made him feel alive and his victims made him feel relevant again, a feeling he hadn't experienced since his dad had died. Even his paranoia was eased, if only temporarily.

It took hours for Joe Lombardi to explain the complexities of his maps to Micko. Eventually Joe used multicolored magic markers to highlight the diagrams. The red marker indicated the danger zones, and Micko wrote the cause of danger in the margins. Yellow marker indicated the locations of various communities, and Micko wrote the name of each communal leader. Green marked active train tunnels and blue marked abandoned tunnels and stations.

Micko checked his pocket watch and realized it was time to check in with the Chief of Detectives. He left his cell phone in the hotel room safe in the Pennsylvania Hotel. He couldn't carry it with him while posing as a homeless unfortunate, and reception underground was impossible.

"Joe, sit here for a while. I'm going to use your directions to find my way back to the waiting room in Penn Station," Micko said.

"Here, take the compass and the chalk, just in case," Joe said.

Micko studied the map and mentally sketched a route. He shook hands with Joe and agreed to meet him at Mr. Waffles' shop later for coffee. The path back was occasionally lit and simple at first. Micko knew he was deep underground and had to climb many levels to reach Penn Station. He daydreamed and swayed his shillelagh as he thought how lucky he was to have two fine places to live in while working undercover in this maze below Manhattan.

Soon, his plain cement-walled tunnel took on a dark, eerie look. The sound of trains racing through active tunnels was unnerving. The tracks that he had been following dead-ended at a collapsed wall. Everything was dilapidated and there were no lights. A howling wind blew newspapers and trash about the debris-covered rails. He checked his compass and he was headed in the right direction. He studied Joe's map again and pictured where he was. He had passed a junction where he needed to climb up through a small grate and gain access to a large abandoned utility room. During his daydreaming, he had walked past the junction and entered one of the red-marked danger zones.

Micko quickly about-faced and walked back to the junction and easily located the vent. He was astonished at how well-lit this new underground cave system was. The grill squealed noisily as he pushed it up and climbed the dirty old ladder rungs. He placed his shillelagh into his belt and climbed about fifty feet until he reached a secondary landing with another grill. He passed through this opening and climbed another set of rusty ladder rungs until he reached a large room through the floor grid.

This huge room looked like it may have once been a power room regulating electricity. The giant generators were covered in grime and obviously out of use for some time.

Micko reviewed his map and knew he had to climb a set of stairs that led to an office complex and pass through an elevator shaft to go up another level. The elevator was long gone, but a set of iron ladder rungs led up the length of the concrete shaft. The map indicated he must climb to the fourth door and exit the shaft. It seemed like every other light bulb was inoperable, as a ghostly hue clouded his vision.

The climb was tiresome, but when he opened the correct door, Micko was astonished to find himself in a well-lit passageway lined with dozens of working steam pipes. It was warm but scary. Every few seconds, steam escaped from various pipes at irregular intervals. The floor was wet and slippery from condensation of the leaking steam.

Micko perused his map to see where he was to go next. It appeared he was on the same level as Penn Station, but he had a long walk along this jungle-like steam pipe complex. As Micko took the long walk, he was shocked that there were no rats along this tube. He smiled to himself as he remembered Joe referring to rats as *track rabbits*.

Eventually Micko arrived at a series of intersecting hallways connected to various shops along the Penn Station Concourse area. Countless belongings of homeless people were scattered about these feces-stained hallways.

Micko exited the putrid-smelling passage between a Dunkin' Donuts and a gift shop. Hundreds of commuters rushed through the concourse en route to work, train, or bus hookups or to shop and sightsee, clueless to the filthy passageways behind the expensive shops lining the same concourse they walked along and shopped in.

Suddenly, Micko saw Blackjack Randazzo roughing up a filthy-looking homeless man. Micko recognized the bum as Slugger O'Toole, a washed-up middleweight boxer. He had a permanently shut right eye due to excessive scarring, which led to his nickname Popeye.

Micko proudly marched through the waiting area of the station and approached Blackjack Randazzo. "Do yer nu who yer are disturbin'? Dis is Slugger O'Toole, yer man knocked oyt Wild Bill Gerhard at de Felt Forum in 1990," Micko said.

"Oh, so the Nutty Irishman is going to give me a boxing history lesson?" Blackjack asked.

Popeye used this interruption to pull away from the bully cop.

"I'm gonna buy dis lad a cup av coffee, if yer don't mind." Micko glared at Randazzo.

There must have been something in the way Micko stared at him that made Blackjack say, "Just stay away from my post."

The two homeless men took a seat at a small table in Dunkin' Donuts as Micko purchased a pair of hot coffees.

"Do I know you?" Popeye cocked his head to the side as he eyeballed Micko.

Micko felt sorry for the punch-drunk man whose glory days were well behind him. He pushed the coffee toward the ex-boxer and smiled.

When he worked the .25 caliber shooter case, Micko had run into the ex-boxer when he was arrested and waiting for transport in a holding cell. In those days, Popeye was known as a cop fighter. If anyone got aggressive with Popeye, there was a fistfight.

Micko had befriended the man whose new fight was with the bottle. He had called one of the outreach groups, after O'Toole was arrested, and one of the group's members helped him out. Popeye was taken to the hospital, cleaned up, and put on a regimen of diazepam for alcohol withdrawals.

Eventually he was placed in an SRO and was doing well for about twenty days. Popeye fell off the wagon, lost his SRO, and was right back where he started. The outreach programs didn't spend much time on two-time losers but spent more time and money on fresh cases that had a potential for better results.

Looking into Popeye's good eye, Micko knew the man had a vague memory of him. He hoped the coffee would make it a good memory.

Micko left the boxer and continued to his secret room. Once inside, he opened the hotel room safe, pulled out the cell phone, and quickly dialed Chief Clifford. "Hello boss. Boy, do I have a lot to tell you."

"Me first," Clifford said.

He informed Micko the other units of the task force were not taking the case seriously. Since there were no bodies or ransom notes, it was being dismissed as simple runaways that didn't deserve serious investigation. There would be no undercover policewoman or additional manpower from the NYPD at Penn Station. "Micko, this guy is not going to stop until you bring him in," the chief said.

"Sir, I'm entrenched both in the underbelly of Penn Station and above. I'm working on visiting underground communities to seek out this miserable bastard."

"Do it quickly, Micko, do it quickly. The newspapers are running the Phantom of Penn Station articles again."

Micko knew he had to devise a plan to capture the madman. Then he remembered the file Captain Pedone had given him regarding the Yonkers murders.

Micko read the report carefully and sat for a long time in a pensive state. He usually did this at homicide scenes he was assigned to investigate. Slowly, the puzzle pieces began to fit into place. The reports indicated Tobias Wilson was a big man, standing 6' 5" and weighing 230 lbs. He was described as having a below-average IQ and homeschooled. Tobias went missing when his mother and lover were discovered dead, both naked except for a red scarf tightly wrapped around the woman's neck.

Franklin Wilson's file revealed he was a senior brakeman and had extensive knowledge of the labyrinth of tunnels and tracks underground, running from Penn Station to Grand Central Station. His file also indicated his son frequently accompanied him to his work assignments in the caves below Manhattan.

Frequently accompanied him to his work assignments!

"That's it! That's the missing piece!" Micko blared to an empty room.

Now Micko realized the only place the lad could hide would be under Penn Station—the same station his father had taught him about.

He grabbed his cell phone again and punched in some numbers from an Amtrak card.

"Hi, Captain Pedone?"

"Yes, who's calling?"

"This is Micko. Can you have one of your men check Franklin Wilson's locker and let me know if anything is missing?"

"Well, like what?"

"Anything that should be there . . . special tools, keys, work clothes, etc."

"All right. I'll go downstairs myself."

"Captain, leave a message on my cell answering machine," Micko said before hanging up.

Micko paced his room, wishing his loyal cat was with him. He was fond of talking his thoughts out loud to his feline pal. He felt less strange when there was another being in the room.

He now knew his enemy and knew he would have to fight in the enemy's territory. Tobias Wilson was most likely traumatized after viewing his father's horrifying death. He had already killed two people in Yonkers and in his twisted mental state was kidnapping red-scarfed women in Penn Station. The victims, dead or alive, were located somewhere in the nether-world beneath him, a netherworld as big as Manhattan itself.

Micko looked at himself in the mirror and smiled at his grubby appearance. The scraggly beard was visible, and the clothes were a mess, especially after Blackjack had wiped sauerkraut and mustard on his coat. Micko had planned to wash up a bit but decided to let it go. He would truly be the Nutty Irishman.

CHAPTER

8

Captain Pedone was pleased to get out of his office for a while. "Larry, man the phones while I'm gone!" he yelled to Sergeant Larry Ayers.

Pedone knew what Micko thought, and now he feared the kidnappings might be real and right under his feet. He walked to the Amtrak dining car service area and took the elevator down three stories. Once he exited the elevator into a chilly, gloomy work zone, he felt unseen eyes studying him from the darkness.

Suddenly a half dozen rats raced across the empty tracks off to his right.

"Goddamn track rabbits! You scared the shit out of me!"

Pedone had been down in these depths before, but not in

a long time and not while a large murderer might be taking refuge. He shook off the willies and walked into the workmen's locker room.

"Hello, Mr. Collins," Pedone said.

"Hi, Richard. What's up?"

"I need to take a look inside Franklin's locker. Can you show me which one is his?"

"Too late. The union guys and the track superintendent already cleared it out."

"Damn. Do you have any idea if there was anything important missing?"

"Sure do. Everyone wanted Franklin's personal maps and sketches. They were gone along with his bag and tools and master keys to places people don't even know exist. I guess Tiny took them right after the accident."

"Who?"

"Tiny, Franklin's son. We affectionately call him Tiny due to his immense size," Mr. Collins said.

Pedone knew this was big trouble. A murderer with knowledge of the underground, possessing tools and master keys. He would have to call the FBI and the Yonkers PD to have a powwow and share this new information to formulate a plan.

Tiny was the Phantom.

Tiny was happy with his new red-scarfed family. They didn't yell at him or tell him to clean his room or do homework. He picked out the movies to show them or played the music he liked. He sneaked up to street level once every couple of days to shake down the more well-to-do panhandlers and pick up supplies.

The paranoia and bad dreams subsided. Adding new members to his growing family seemed to be the answer. He also loved the adrenaline rush after tricking the police and snatching a victim from right under their patrols.

Rearranging his ladies in this lair was an exercise he enjoyed. These victims were his Barbie Dolls. Sometimes he removed their overcoats and stared at them in their dresses or street clothes. He felt a strange excitement while looking at his ladies. Being an unintelligent young man, he didn't understand the warm glow that overcame his senses as he touched the women.

Sometimes he placed one on the bed and two at the small coffee table. Then the next day he would rearrange them in another pattern. This entertained him during the day along with his movies and music.

He knew he must add to his family while being watchful of police activity in and around Penn Station. His need for more red-scarfed Barbie Dolls outweighed his fear of the police. Tiny began to plan new diversions for grabbing his ladies.

Micko stealthily left his secret room and exited Penn Station. He enjoyed the crisp, cold breeze coming off the Hudson River as he walked to Mr. Waffles. Joe the Gimp was engaged in a lively conversation with a number of homeless when he spotted Micko. "And here is the hero now!" he proudly exclaimed.

The undercover detective had to snap back to decoy mode. "Waaat ye blatherin' about, boyo?"

"You're all the underground citizens are talking about. Even Hannity wants to meet you. Of all the women bums to stand up for, you picked the most popular." He smiled.

Micko motioned toward a distant table and Joe gave an understanding nod.

"Joe, do you or any of the underground dwellers know a big, senseless kid named Tobias?"

"Sure everyone knows Tiny. He used to work with his father coupling and uncoupling subway cars. Now we hear he may be hiding out down in the lower levels. We don't know why, but he has put the fear of God into some of the bullshit panhandlers on Eighth Avenue."

"What do you mean bullshit panhandlers?"

"Shit, every year at Christmastime well-to-do people come down here from the suburbs and act like poor beggars and make big bucks. Local bums act crazy, curse, and are drunk. The phonies are good actors and act nice but needy. The generous people feel sorrier for the actors than the real destitute. We have seen these people beg all day, then get picked up in expensive cars and go home. Tiny knows this and shakes them down for protection money."

"Damn, I am really getting a life lesson while working down here. Try not to call me by my name when we are in public. Remember, I'm the Nutty Irishman!"

"Listen, a couple of the indigents that are members of Hannity's Rats were here earlier, and he has extended an invitation to meet you," Joe said.

"Well, let's not keep him waiting."

"Look at the map I gave you and lead the way. It's clearly marked as Hannity's Manor," Joe said.

Micko viewed the map and made a silent calculation then said, "We're off to see the Wizard, the wonderful Wizard of Oz."

The duo walked around the corner to 4 Pennsylvania Avenue and entered Penn Station next to Madison Square Garden. As they walked down the stairs, an old bag lady screeched, "Bakala!"

"What the hell does that mean?" Micko asked Joe.

"No one knows. We call her Grandma Bakala. She shouts at people and they feel sorry and give her loose coins. Bag ladies live in the nooks and crannies of tunnels that run through the street level where Madison Square Garden meets Penn Station."

Micko led the way to a hallway that corkscrewed under Madison Square Garden. The passage dead-ended at a large boiler room, and Micko lifted the metal grate cover to reveal a set of stairs that also corkscrewed down below.

They went down four levels. Madison Square Garden was built above the old Penn Station, and they climbed down past several abandoned train stations. The stairwell was dimly lit and the stairs were slippery from a steady flow of water seeping through the porous walls.

When they reached a landing at the bottom, Micko shined his flashlight into the huge, pitch-black tunnel ahead. Then he flashed it onto his map to get his bearings. This enormous corridor was lightless. Micko looked at Joe and Joe just tilted his head toward the gigantic passageway.

Micko's senses were on full alert. The walls were fifty feet apart and a trough of running water ran in the center of the chasm between two sets of abandoned tracks. Water sloshed against their feet. Slowly they walked as their flashlight beams pierced the inky darkness. Track rabbits scurried out of their way as they ambled through. There was a complete absence of sound, except Micko's heart beating so loud he feared it would warn enemies of his approach.

Eventually, they came to a cave-like intersection. One tunnel went east and one went west. Micko knew that the west hallway went to the Hudson River so he went east.

The pair walked in total silence for what seemed like a great distance until the floor became dry and every once in a while there was a wall light bulb to help navigate through the gloom. Even the noisy sound of freight and subway trains bustling through active tunnels was welcomed.

Micko finally asked, "How far do we have to go?"

"Everywhere underground is a long and arduous journey. That's why only the strong survive down here," Joe replied with a seriousness in his voice.

As they continued, the lighting became better and the way clearer. Soon they could hear noise from up ahead as the tunnel widened like a funnel. The passageways' walls became pockmarked with chasms and smaller hallways leading away from this main artery.

Suddenly, five men appeared from one of the larger tributaries, brandishing club-like weapons. Micko and Joe froze. The centurions gave the interlopers a good once over, then a muscular man asked, "Are you the Nutty Irishman?"

"Of course he is, you fools. We were invited. Now take us to Hannity!" Joe bellowed at the ragtag army of tramps.

One of the centurions recognized Joe and said, "You better be careful, Gimp."

Micko and Joe were led through a labyrinth of corridors, all showing signs of life in a well-lit community. Women hung laundry on clotheslines, others cooked over small fires as children stared at the newcomers.

This settlement was home to Hannity's Rats. Micko's mind raced. *Who would have thought that people lived like this under the very streets of downtown Manhattan?*

"You must be the Nutty Irishman," a small, impish man said in a low voice.

Micko nodded. Joe had warned him about smiling and showing his perfect teeth or talking too much in his horrible Irish.

"I'm Hannity, and these are my people. Welcome to Hannity's Manor."

Micko looked at the little man with the disheveled gray beard and dark piercing eyes. The man resembled Charles Manson.

"We all owe you a debt of gratitude for saving Miss Kitty. You are the talk of all the underground societies and all the mayors wish to meet you," Hannity said. "Come, come I will show you our communal lifestyle."

"This is Jersey Jack. He is my chief centurion. He and his men protect our community from the subhuman scum who would steal from us and rape our women."

Micko nodded at the muscular man who had approached them earlier.

Hannity led the way with Jersey Jack and his band of vigilantes following at a discreet distance.

Hannity crouched through a narrow wall opening and exited into a colossal, high-ceilinged, stone-walled cathedral as large as Penn Station's waiting room. Micko and Joe had to crouch through the opening but were surprised at the scene portrayed before them.

Small bungalow huts scattered about everywhere with the chaotic activities of an undersized renaissance village. Little children, cats, dogs, and potbellied pigs added an asylum atmosphere to the settlement.

With opened arms, Hannity cried out, "Bear witness to our madness!"

Hannity looked Micko directly in the eye and said, "We live in a socialist commune. Everyone shares and receives from the population."

Dozens of fires were contained in 55 gallon drums providing both light and warmth. Each hovel was lined with lanterns so the community was well lit as the peasants gleefully performed their daily tasks.

Along a huge expanse of wall, Hannity pointed out gorgeous murals painted by graffiti artists with inscriptions portrayed between paintings.

Micko stopped to admire one. *It's our mistakes and the way we correct them that define us.*

Two men approached as Micko admired the graffiti-covered wall.

"This is Mango and Bevo, our esteemed artists," Hannity said.

Both men were too hygienic to be citizens of this underworld existence, and Micko gave them the obvious look over.

"Our artistic friends are from above. Their creative juices have no boundaries and they are always welcome to visit here to paint their imagination on our walls for all to see," Hannity said.

Micko once again nodded his approval and waved his shillelagh in the direction of a huge tent structure.

"This is the community brothel. Most women live with a man, but once a month each male member of the village barters with the women for relief of biological tension buildup," Hannity said.

Joe tried to stifle a chuckle but failed.

"This is Hairy Mary. She is in charge of the bordello and acts as a liaison during the bartering to make sure all are in agreement," Hannity said.

Micko imagined how she got her name. Mary was hairy—arms, neck, and upper lip—all hairy. Being of stocky build didn't help her overall appearance.

He nodded and gave a slight bow to Hairy Mary and they moved on to another part of the hamlet.

While Micko had yet to utter a word, Hannity was an insatiable orator. The decoy cop learned all about Hannity's Rats. To keep the Amtrak Police at bay, Hannity's Raiders conducted daily sweeps of the platforms located in the Eye of the Needle. Crack addicts were ushered out from below the platforms. Coconut Head was the leader of these vagrant vigilantes.

Hannity proudly declared, "After Coconut Head and my raiders complete their rounds, they always return to the womb."

Micko thought this eerie scene looked reminiscent of seventh-century serfdom. Hannity acted as the lord of the manor and his centurions and raiders became the knights protecting the peasants of this feudalistic colony. Those who didn't adhere to Hannity's harsh rules were considered vagabonds and kicked out of the village to live farther below in other underground communities.

Hannity introduced Micko to the Fat Man, who was in charge of food distribution among the serfs. Each peasant had a specific job and was rewarded accordingly.

"Cotton Top, this is the Nutty Irishman that everyone is talking about," Hannity said.

Micko lowered his head and gently shook her dainty hand. She was about forty years old with shockingly white hair that resembled a Q-tip. She was a pretty woman, more hygienic than the others.

Joe whispered, "Her real name is Doris T, and she is an actual nurse. Some topside tragedy caused her to leave her name and career behind as she became a Mole Person."

"Cotton Top is the head nurse who runs my hospital and delivers all the newborns," Hannity said.

Before Micko could ask a question, Hannity answered it as he continuously crowed about his beloved commune.

"Cotton Top gives monthly checkups to the women who work in the brothel and check for obvious signs of STDs. The men are also checked just prior to any activity within the brothel. Rooster and other topside runners provide condoms in an attempt to prevent the spread of sexually transmitted diseases."

Micko also learned that when a member of the colony died or when the Hannity Raiders discovered a dead body, the corpse was dropped down the Waste Way.

Joe asked, "The what?"

Hannity grinned and motioned for the two guests to follow him. "We have people of all classes dying down here all the time. My colonists, thieves, and vagabonds that kill each other for food, women, or drugs. Sometimes newcomers get lost in the maze of tunnels and starve. Others just lose the will to live. Here we are banned by society. Unwanted and homeless, we become a breed apart, nomads who scorn the aboveground laws, so we are forced to enforce our own."

After walking past the village to a rear subterranean compartment, Hannity pointed to a pit with a narrow airshaft.

"We drop the dearly departed down this shaft that falls to the bedrock far below. We have a simple service and drop during low tide. The cadaver falls into a shallow aqueduct and is eaten by rats. We dispose of human waste and trash the same way. When the tide changes, the remains are washed out into the Hudson River."

"I've heard that the Morlocks also feast on the dead bodies," Joe said.

Micko shot Joe an inquisitive glance.

"The Morlock Nation live in the absolute lowest levels of Manhattan. The Mole People call it the No Zone. They have been living there, evolving for hundreds of years. Expelled by humanity for various reasons, they sought refuge underground and live a primitive lifestyle," Joe said.

Hannity added, "These airshafts have been built over the course of construction and renovations for about two hundred years. The sandhogs needed these airshafts to breathe while they worked and raised the railroad structure higher and higher."

Micko realized how crude, yet efficient, this process of eliminating all human waste was. *How long has this been going on?*

Hannity made a motion to follow him again. The self-proclaimed lord of the manor led his guests through a wet, dingy corridor that sloped down toward an abandoned railroad tunnel. The train tracks ran downward through this channel and abruptly stopped at a dead-end where the wall had collapsed, forming an impassable barricade. An elaborate row of derelict shacks lined each side of the railroad tracks, forming an unconventional shantytown.

"This is where my exiled vagrants live. I excommunicated them from my humble village because they either violated my laws or were too uncontrollable. We all have a healthy disdain for rules, but robberies, rape, thefts, and drug and alcohol abuse are rampant among these Mole People of Shantytown. See all the catacombs that lead into this tunnel? This is where the community mayors come for formal meetings to discuss shared problems," Hannity said.

Joe explained, "Sometimes a rogue mole will savagely run amuck, causing chaos within the communities. Other times a displaced gang will do the same. Runners are sent to the community mayors informing them of a meeting here to determine how to resolve the problem. These catacomb tributaries run throughout the underground world and provide easy access for the leaders."

Hannity continued, "Each community has a police force. I have my raiders, the Vietnam Vets have the Outfit, and so on. We hunt down the violators and they meet the Waste Way."

Micko's head reeled from an overload of information. He had trouble comprehending everything revealed to him. He feared he might wind up becoming a nutty Irishman.

The undercover cop gave a subtle pre-arranged nod to Joe.

"The Nutty Irishman doesn't speak much, but he is livid about locating Tiny. The big oaf stole something that he desperately wants returned."

Hannity replied, "I have heard that Tiny is wandering the upper halls and shaking down the bag people impersonators above. If it is that important I will call a general meeting of mayors and send out search parties."

Micko stared Hannity directly in the eye and said, "I tanks Mr. 'annity."

On the way back to the humongous cathedral where Hannity's Rats lived, the lord of the manor spoke incessantly about his love for his village and serfs. He also justified his underground lifestyle.

Hannity believed the aboveground world was in peril. He repeated warnings from noted theoretical physicist, Stephen Hawking. He believed the planet Earth was long overdue for another asteroid strike. Such a strike could wipe out mankind or at the very best send humans back to prehistoric times.

The lord of the manor was also concerned with the overpopulation of the planet. He rambled about Earth's resources being limited and if the exploitation of these resources didn't cease, humans risked the calamity of deadly weather deviations.

Micko watched as Hannity's face reddened and his temperament evolved into restrained madness. His eyes widened and glowed like hot coals as he continued about his concerns over the effect a solar explosion, flare, or storm could have on humanity.

Hannity held his hands to his head and blurted, "Climate change, over population, pandemics, and our warring ways will get us in the end! Living below in our catacombs will be our salvation. When life above dies, people will rush below to become Mole People, so we are preparing our defenses."

As a film of saliva slid down the left side of Hannity's mouth, Micko realized the man was mad as a hatter. His fears were justified, but his obsession was pure madness.

As soon as the trio returned to the calmness of the Renaissance Village, Hannity concluded his raving lunacy and said, "Of course, you two will always have a place at my table."

The graffiti artists, Mango and Bevo approached and asked, "Do you want to see our latest creation?"

"Yes, please take us there," Hannity said, as he returned to his subdued nature.

The artists led the way through a hole in a wall that corkscrewed through a darkened labyrinth of interconnected grottoes. The walls were covered with bright-colored murals from previous accomplishments.

After passing several wall paintings, the pair of artists stopped in front of a huge portraiture depicting a modern-day Sodom and Gomorrah with an underground setting.

Naked men and women entangled in sexual positions spilling wine from goblets were spread out on railroad tracks. Goblins rose from the chimneys of tiny shacks with a huge, red, menacing devil hovering above. Bloody, dismembered bodies scattered the tracks with naked nymphs laughing at the carnage.

"Well, what do you think? This is our greatest creation and it only took two weeks to complete," Bevo said.

Micko looked on in horror as he observed the ghastly images. Joe's expression was indifferent.

"What do you call it?" Hannity asked, euphorically.

Mango answered proudly, "The permissive nature of man!"

Captain Pedone nervously paced in his office waiting for Micko to return his call. He had already telephoned his contacts in the FBI task force and his Amtrak superiors. He gave them an update on his progress with the missing persons of interest. The others were still in denial that there was anything amiss.

"How many other missing persons do you have for this month?" asked Amtrak supervisor Steve Wallace.

"Six so far," Pedone replied.

"Well, when you get twelve, we'll get concerned!"

"But boss, those other 'missings' are already classified as run-aways, druggies, and family related. These two women point to a problem, especially with Tobias Wilson thrown into the mix," an exasperated Pedone explained.

"What did the FBI say?" Wallace demanded.

After a short pause he replied, "They feel the same as you. No bodies, no ransom, no case."

"Well then, pass off this Wilson kid to the Yonkers cops as the Phantom, and keep that station good and secure with Christmas right around the corner," Wallace said and hung up.

CHAPTER

9

Tiny was very happy living in his new world. Each morning he played rap music while he showered and shaved in the warmth and comfort of Tiny's Place. After dressing in clean clothes, he made a cup of coffee for himself and tea for his lady guests in the cooler.

He sat and talked to them for hours. They never yelled at him or used disparaging remarks like his mother had done. Tiny was extremely pleased with his newest lady. She was young, pretty, and shapely. He always sat next to her when he visited his lodgers.

Tiny immediately cleaned his visitors of postmortem defecation, but even in the confines of the freezer, the smell of death was apparent. He wanted to raise the temperature to refrigeration status since his ladies were dripping icicles, hindering their facial features. He knew this might slowly increase decomposition, but he decided to chance it to keep his women pretty.

The Daniel Boone of the netherworld realized he had become too lax in his hiding when he was recognized aboveground one night. Tiny wanted a fresh hot dog from Hawkeye at the Papaya King kiosk, but before he got close, Rooster locked eyes with him.

Tiny knew Rooster was one of the most trustworthy runners to the underground communities and now his presence would soon be known to all the Mole People. He had to move his shopping area outside the realm of snooping eyes. He needed hygiene products for himself and his ladies. Tiny decided they should all smell like his mother, so he purchased a case of cheap perfume. He also bought a case of olive oil. He remembered watching a television show with his father about Egyptian mummies. The TV announcer explained how the ancients used olive oil to help preserve the decaying skin of the pharaohs.

Soon Tiny had the temperature in the cooler at a pleasant, cool setting and he undressed and bathed his tenants in olive oil with a splash of fragrance. He always returned a clean red scarf around their dainty necklines. This undressing was difficult since each corpse went through varying degrees of rigor mortis.

Mary the Man sold flowers on Ninth Avenue, and Tiny wanted to purchase a vase of flowers to place on the small coffee table in the freezer room for his ladies.

Mary was a large woman wearing a green coat and a green wool cap.

"Mary, what kind of flowers are those?" Tiny asked, as he pointed to a poinsettia plant.

"What are you, stupid, or did you just fall off a turnip truck?" she mocked in a deep voice.

"Fall off the what? Why do they call you Mary the Man?" he asked innocently.

Angrily, Mary reached behind her chair and pulled out an ugly piece of lead pipe. With that, the wide-eyed Tiny left hastily to Tenth Avenue. Here an old man sold the same pretty red flowers.

Without much conversation, Tiny purchased two of the holiday plants. *At least I won't have to buy a vase*, he chuckled to himself.

When Tiny surreptitiously returned to Tiny's Place, he presented the pair of flower pots to his trio of comely dames. "An early Christmas present to my lovelies," he proudly declared.

He already had his latest conquest seated at the small table, so he went to the bed where the other two were perched. Soon Tiny and his three ladies were seated at the table with one set of flowers between them and the other on the bed nightstand.

Tiny told his women about the daily dangers he faced, and since he was recognized by the enemy, he must take greater precautions in the future. When Mary the Man had produced the lead pipe to threaten him, Tiny knew he must carry protection himself. The halogen tool that was partly responsible for his father's death would be his armament.

Now, when Tiny ventured aboveground, he secured his weapon under his large black-hooded overcoat for concealment. Tiny was careful to find new locations to shop and before long, was comfortable on the far west side. The bag ladies, runners, and occasional Mole People never risked leaving the safety of the immediate perimeter of Penn Station. They knew the stores and the stores knew them. It was an unholy alliance but an alliance. The shopkeepers made a lot of money on the hapless homeless people.

Since Tiny didn't appear as wretched as the other poor derelicts, he could shop anywhere. Living in Tiny's Place allowed him to wash himself and his clothes, giving him a decent appearance. He paid with cash, so nobody questioned his motives.

During one of his late-night exploration forays, Tiny came upon a deserted railroad line that was not on his father's map. This excited him and he followed it deep underground until it dead-ended where a tunnel wall had collapsed onto the tracks.

He reached a tattered door, entered, and followed the ancient hallway into a room where a large aqueduct of water collected. The offensive odors were overwhelming. Tiny spotted another small archway that led out of the aqueduct into a huge cavern. The floor was covered in a brownish dust and had a strong smell of salt water.

The giant dungeon had several doorways sealed with concrete that was newer than the other surroundings. Then Tiny remembered a story his father had told him.

"Son, in ancient times, smugglers would steal from boats along the Hudson River and hide the contraband in a huge cavern. There they would split the booty and find buyers before moving the contraband out. This went on for many years, and when the railroad was built along the Hudson River, modifications were made so that a ramp extended from the cave to the railroad tracks. Contraband would be removed from special freight cars and transported to Smugglers' Cove. Eventually the authorities found out and sealed all of the escape routes from the cove."

This explained the newer mortar on the sealed-off doorways. He walked to the thick concrete ramp and followed it to where it dropped off a few feet above the Hudson Line train tracks. This spot was not easily accessible by foot, so nobody would even know it was there.

Tiny imagined that during prohibition, booze was transported by freight trains from Canada to this spot and offloaded from boxcars. He imagined the criminals would have used a wooden ramp running from the boxcar to the cove's concrete ramp and then rolled into the hidden cove.

He walked back into the giant dungeon but did not want to go back into the smelly aqueduct. He searched for a way around the putrid water and found a rusty old sewer line that fed deeper underground, running parallel to the cove's ramp.

Tiny used his small but powerful flashlight to guide him through the dark, murky sewer pipe. The pipe was only four feet high, so Tiny had to crouch down to navigate through it. The rats here were much bigger than the ones he had previously encountered. *These track rabbits must be river rats.*

These larger rats were unafraid, and Tiny had to kick them out of his way, otherwise he feared he would stumble into the rancid sewage. Suddenly, Tiny glimpsed a lighter hue appearing as he neared the sewer exit.

The gutter deposited him right under the Hudson Freight Line railroad tracks, a few dozen yards from the river itself. Tiny never knew this sewer system existed or led to this coveted spot. He was now lower than the concrete ramp leading to Smugglers' Cove.

Tiny looked up and a cliff of bedrock rose above him. Below he could see a slight drop-off past the train tracks. This drop-off led down to the banks of the Hudson River. Tiny sat on a little bluff overlooking this magnificent view. There were no lights here, so he could see the overhead stars clearly. He felt safe and knew he would return here again. He wished he could bring his favorite kidnap victim here to see the sights.

All was right in Tiny's world. He found new places to shop. His women were clean and perfumed. Their room was cool but comfortable and had flowers. He was mastering the vast confines of his netherworld and scouting out new places.

Micko and Joe both left Hannity and his village badly needing a shower. This they agreed on as they spoke about the surreal community of Hannity's Rats. A few years earlier, Joe was an occasional visitor to the commune. Hannity found Joe to be sensible, clean, and a well-respected and dec-orated soldier. Joe took advantage of the brothel, the library, and the routine hospital checkups.

Since both Joe and Hannity were educated, they had lively, intelligent conversations. It took Joe a few months to realize Hannity was insane. Hannity's rules didn't apply to everyone and enforcement was selective. Drinking and drugging were not permitted, but visiting mayors and staff would drink and do drugs in private with Hannity.

If anyone else was caught drinking, Hannity would have them publicly flogged in the village square. Moose was his main enforcer, devoted to inflicting pain.

Some drinkers were banished to the horrors of Shantytown while others were treated for their affliction. Various social outreach groups provided condoms, medicines, and pills for anti-abuse of alcohol. Selective punishment scared Joe, but it was the gun incident that scared him the most.

One day Hannity complained about a lone wolf nomad terrifying a community run by the Mighty Quinn. This nomad stabbed several tribe members and raped and badly injured a woman. Various community police groups were unable to capture him before he raped and killed Papa Miller's daughter. Papa was the well-respected mayor of the Lost Souls' community in the extremely low levels of Grand Central Station.

That day, Hannity flashed a small gun during his tirade and threatened to kill anyone who gave safe harbor to the rapist murderer. Guns were virtually absent underground unless law-evading gangs sought temporary refuge. Even then, they were frowned upon. For Hannity to not only possess one but publicly display it was cause for concern. Joe never returned until today.

Micko and Joe enjoyed their conversation and walk home and parted at the 34th Street and Eighth Avenue entrance to Penn Station. Joe was going to his SRO apartment to take a nice, hot shower and wash off the imaginary parasites that made him itch. Micko laughed and said he would do the same, but a long bath was in order.

"Remember, no smelly soap," Joe reminded with a laugh. "You're still the undercover Nutty Irishman."

Micko went down a flight of stairs to a lower level and worked his way to the hidden elevator room. He threw on the power and took the ride to his secret hotel room. He immediately drew a hot bath, dropped his clothes on the floor, and hopped in.

Although he wore warm clothing, after many hours in the underground world, he caught a chill. *Or is it from viewing the Waste Way and Shantytown?* Nestled in the opulence of the hotel's hot bath, Micko analyzed all he had learned. *Why is it that thinking is easier and everything so much clearer in a bath?*

His thoughts ran wild as he comprehended the complexities of this case. Apparently a troubled youth was present when his father was killed during a horrific accident on an unused subway line. The poor kid ran home to tell his mother and found her in bed with the neighbor's son. This made the youth unravel and he used his immense size to strangle them.

Micko paused, then continued to reconstruct the past few days' events. The boy fled his Westchester home and raided his father's utility locker in Penn Station and took up residence in the depths of Penn Station. For some reason, his demented mind pushed him to kidnap women in red that reminded him of his mother's red scarf-crested neck. The strong, slow-witted youngster was also very familiar with the spider web of tunnels, abandoned underground warehouses, and communities. This left Micko and the police at a great disadvantage. The netherworld below NYC streets went down many levels and ran for many, many miles from Manhattan all the way up to the Bronx.

He added more hot water to his tub and continued his mental reenactment of recent events.

Unbelievable communities lived in the underworld dungeons and they lived like serfs from the Middle Ages. He had only visited one community, and he could only wonder what the other communities were like.

The now-refreshed detective checked his cell phone and viewed a number of stories and schematics detailing the underground history of Penn Station, courtesy of Esmeralda. Before he dove into this reading material, he realized he had a message from Captain Pedone. Micko played back the message.

"Micko, you are on your own down there. I made all of the proper notifications regarding Tobias Wilson, the red scarf, and the connection to the women dressed in red missing from Penn

Station where we know Tobias is hiding. He is our Phantom of Penn Station. The Yonkers Police will not come down here to look for him in the underground maze. They just posted a wanted card on him. They hope that Tobias gets arrested on another charge and when he is booked, the wanted card will pop up. Then they will appear at court and arrest him for the West-chester murders.

"They are taking the easy way out. The FBI will only take a wait-and-see attitude since there are many missings this time of year and no bodies or ransom notes have been produced. The Amtrak supervisors do not want any negative attention during the holiday season, so I am ordered to merely keep the station secure. Sorry buddy. Text me if you want me to come to your room to powwow."

This was a major problem Micko had not anticipated. It took almost a full hour to bring Chief Clifford up to date. He was furious. The purpose of a task force was because no single agency had the manpower to handle complex cases such as this. The chief didn't have any men to spare. This was Christmas week and his men were spread thin trying to do anti-terrorist duties, anti-crime duties, and the everyday work an overworked detective normally handled. No bodies meant no undercover policewoman as bait. He didn't like the idea of the media stirring things up with wild phantom accusations.

"Micko, stay on this and I'll owe you big time. If bodies start to appear, we will all be in the shithouse. Remember, you are on the clock twenty-four hours a day until you catch this prick. Your reward will be a promotion to second grade detective and a ton of overtime. Now hang up the phone and get back to work!"

Micko smiled as he hung up the cell phone. Chief Clifford sounded like he was unraveling. He grabbed a cold beer from the mini fridge and studied the material Esmeralda had sent him. Armed with this new info and Joe's maps, he felt confident he could tackle the behemoth cave system that twisted far below the busy streets of Manhattan. He now knew he would not have any other police help. His only source of help capturing the Phantom would be from homeless degenerates, vagrants, lunatics, druggies, and an overabundance of losers that called subterranean sewers their home.

When they were last together, Esmeralda had packed him a knapsack with a variety of things that cave explorers carried and insisted Micko take it with him. He decided he should now carry this backpack in case he got lost, thirsty, hungry, or injured.

Tiny was so relaxed looking over the peaceful Hudson River that even the brisk air couldn't keep him from drifting off into sleep. He didn't know what made him awake with a start, but he accidentally pushed some loose stones with his feet and they tumbled down the small hill to the riverbed below. One rock landed on something solid and produced a weird sound. Most of the rocks slid down on soil and other rocks, but Tiny thought one rock landed on a hidden pipe.

It was still very dark, so Tiny used his flashlight to climb down the slope. Once he reached the foot of the hill, he carefully looked around. He saw an ancient water tunnel pipe barely breaching the foot of the hill. He took a closer look and observed that the inside of the pipe was four feet wide and four feet high, and rancid water spilled out and into the river below. Amazingly, this pipe ran even farther under the railroad tracks he had been sitting next to.

Tiny was shocked that this pipe came from a region lower than the bedrock. He didn't think anything was lower than the tube he had exited from earlier. This meant there was yet another lower labyrinth of tunnels and corridors he was unaware of. This pleased him as he had visions of new explorations as Daniel Boone.

Tiny was tired and decided to return to Tiny's Place to tell his women about his new discovery.

CHAPTER

10

It was now nighttime and Micko was hungry, so he took a walk to see Hawkeye at the Papaya King stand and ask if he had seen Joe.

"No, I haven't seen Joe, but Rooster is looking for you. He has information on the Phantom. That's what the newspapers are calling Tiny," Hawkeye explained.

"Where 'ill oi fend Rooster?" he asked in his Nutty Irishman speech.

"He should be at the St. Agnes soup kitchen on Tenth Avenue," Hawkeye replied.

Micko walked the few blocks in the chilly night air and was happy the soup kitchen was heated. There was a long line waiting to be served, and Micko took this time to look the place over. He placed his shillelagh between his belt loops and rubbed his hands to warm them.

It saddened the hardened detective to see the anguish on the faces of these homeless beggars sitting despairingly at weathered tables. Some despots ate heartily while others made groaning sounds and others just stared into space, lost in their psychotic thoughts. Filthy garments hung off the thin limbs of these bag people. One thing they all had in common was that they all appeared to be nervous and fidgety. Even the Mole People wanted nothing to do with them.

Most of the beggars were loners that sat shivering, even though the soup kitchen was heated. *Someone has to do something for these poor people,* Micko thought. He knew there should be adequate help for the mentally ill, the alcoholics, and the drug addicts. There were institutions that could help these people, but only if they were able to seek out the help themselves. Most of the organizations were flawed. Homeless people were directed to these administrations by well-intentioned social workers, but the homeless often went once and never returned due to dangerous and rundown conditions in so-called safe houses and shelters. In reality, there wasn't much hope for the destitute in NYC.

He saw several nuns dishing out the food from behind a long row of weathered, fold-up tables. A pair of large men in cook outfits stood at either end of the serving line, presumably to keep the peace.

Micko covertly looked at the vagrants sitting at old, worn, wooden picnic tables eating their meals. He observed similar groups ate together but didn't mingle with the others.

When Micko moved up in line to the first nun, she smiled and placed a large piece of homemade bread onto his plate.

The next nun splashed out a stew substance onto his plate along with a scoop of boiled potatoes. The final nun handed out one of those small milk containers schoolchildren drink.

"Help yourself to the coffee and tea along that wall," one of the giant cooks grunted.

Micko looked in that direction and spotted Rooster waving at him. The hungry detective sat at a half-full table next to the underground runner. Rooster smiled and they ate in silence for several minutes.

Soon many of the unfortunates finished eating and returned to their home . . . the streets. Seeing this, Rooster said, "Let's move over to that empty table where we can have some privacy."

When they moved and settled in, Rooster said, "I have word that Tiny is definitely living below and is moving about. I saw him last night at street level, but my sources have seen him deep underground. Tiny is fairly clean and groomed, so he must have a special place underground. I will be visiting all the underground mayors and arranging a meeting, so we can organize a vigilante patrol to flush him out of his subterranean lair. The local media are saying that the Phantom of Penn Station is lurking underground. Is Tiny the Phantom?"

Micko nodded no, when suddenly Kitty walked up and gently kissed him on the cheek as she placed her tiny milk container on his plate.

"Oh, that's not necessary, Miss Kitty," he said.

"Give my best to Joe," she whispered as she walked out into the frigid night.

"Women. Always interrupting. Now where was I?" Rooster asked.

"Do yer organize vigilantes often?" Micko asked.

"Every once in a while criminals seek shelter underground while they hide from the police. If that Amtrak cop Blackjack Randazzo comes to us for help, we put together a vigilante search party. Blackjack is tough on the bag people that loiter in Penn Station's lobby, but he's cool with us if we stay out of sight. When the suspects are caught, the team leader, Senior, duct tapes the fugitive to the lamppost on the corner of 34th Street and Eighth Avenue. One of the runners goes to the Amtrak Police Station in Penn Station and alerts the cops. The fugitive is arrested and the cops leave us alone and help us with health issues such as lice. Senior has been the vigilante team leader for many years and this system works well."

Micko nodded his approval but was silently astounded. Duct tape worked as well, if not better, than handcuffs. *What a sight it must be as Amtrak cops cut a perpetrator from a lamppost and haul his sorry ass to jail.*

Just then a group of scraggly undernourished youths warily entered the soup kitchen and waited their turn in line. Some appeared to be as young as ten or eleven years old. It looked like a scene out of Oliver Twist and Micko wondered, *Which one is the pickpocket known as the Artful Dodger?*

Micko silently nodded toward them and Rooster said, "They're runaways that live under the rotunda in Riverside Park."

Joe had already told Micko about these homeless kids and their leader Ali, but he wanted to know more so he raised his eyebrows while staring at Rooster.

With a sigh Rooster continued. "Ali is the mayor of the Rotunda Kids and he keeps them as safe as possible and off drugs. There's only three ways into their community. One is through a large tunnel past The Hanoi Hotel and the Vietnam Vets, and that ain't happening. As crazy and morally aberrant as they are, they protect the kids. The second, and most common entrance, is through a secret underground grating in Riverside Park. The third way of entry is from the Hudson River banks. A difficult climb over a twenty-five-foot fence, then cross the railroad tracks and into a dangerous sewer canal system loaded with big rats. Recently, a handful of Crips gang members stumbled upon the secret street-level grating and seriously injured two of the Rotunda Kids. Ali now has the grating locked shut with a heavy-duty chain and lock, so all members must use the third way in and out."

Micko listened intently and thought, *What the hell planet am I living on?*

Rooster took a long sip from his coffee. Micko nodded to indicate he wanted more information.

"We don't ask the Rotunda moles to join our vigilantes because most of them are just kids, and the older ones are needed there to protect them. The Hanoi Hilton vets will not help us search for wanted criminals but will help when one of our own goes rogue and starts killing, robbing, and raping. This is the law of the land down there."

While Micko digested this new information, two brutish street bums approached a table where a small group of Rotunda squatters sat. The youngsters' eyes widened as they froze in their seats. He couldn't hear what the vagrants said, but he knew they terrorized the teens.

Wordlessly, he pulled the shillelagh from his waistband, walked to the teens' table, and crashed the head of the ugly stick directly in front of the pair of would-be robbers. A very short staring contest ensued as the hoboes mumbled under their breath and left the shelter.

"The Nutty Irishman!" one of the teenagers cried out.

Micko gave a short nod and walked back to his table with Rooster. Micko was quickly learning how to communicate through gestures, grunts, and body language.

Rooster brought back two fresh cups of coffee and grinned. "You are quickly becoming the Marshal Dillon of the Mole People. That was Spic and Span. They are brothers who are notorious for robbing unfortunates. They usually hide under the train platforms and rob the junkies. They steal clothing, drugs, jewelry, and anything they can get their hands on. I'll be the most popular runner in the underground world when I tell the secret societies that I witnessed this defiant act. I can tell the story as I seek out the mayors for the big meeting."

"Spic an' Span?" Micko asked.

"Well, you saw how filthy they are. Some genius came up with those names to mock them. Pretty clever, wouldn't you say?"

Micko caught himself at the last second as he was about to flash a wide smile. His pearly whites would have blown his cover. This Rooster was a pretty clever fellow himself, too smart to be a mere runner for underground moles.

Rooster was all caffeinated up and couldn't stop talking. Micko directed the conversation and learned the Vietnam Vets were aware of his saving Miss Kitty and should be receptive to him if he visited. They also had misfits amongst them called the Section 8s. While The Hanoi Hilton was a pretty nice place to live, the Section 8s lived along abandoned railroad tracks in filthy dilapidated shacks and lean-tos. In addition, if a Section 8 wore any part of a military uniform, he had to have a red number eight sown on the outermost garment for all to see.

Micko learned the separate groups of vets lived in the same abandoned train tunnel, but that's about all they shared. The Hell's Kitchen neighborhood had several soup kitchens, and the two groups never went to the same one. The Mighty Quinn was the current leader of The Hanoi Hilton. The Section 8s were leaderless.

Rooster went on and on, but when Micko tried to direct the conversation toward the Morlock Nation, he suddenly clammed up. He abruptly looked very uncomfortable and wouldn't make eye contact.

Micko pulled out his shillelagh and smacked it hard on top of the table nearly spilling their coffees.

"I've told people about the Morlocks and they don't believe me, so I don't ever speak of them. We all know of their existence, but very few have ever seen them and none have ever spoken to them. Except me," Rooster stammered.

Rooster was in obvious distress as he looked nervously over his shoulder and around the room. Slowly he continued. "I have been a runner for a long time and make a decent living at it. I live aboveground and eat well. I tried to expand my client list to those troglodytes who live in the very bottommost level of the caves. At first I only met them in absolute darkness. They have really bastardized the English language and have added in squeaks, grunts, and shrilly cries as part of their communication. Eventually, I caught on and traded clothing, sunglasses, and candles for the freshest oysters in New York. I sold the oysters to restaurants and made a small fortune."

The beleaguered runner took another sip of coffee. "I first met them by accident. I was picking up expired sandwiches from the Amtrak food coaches, when I saw an employee take an old dilapidated elevator to lower floors. I waited ten minutes, then pressed for the elevator to return. When I entered the machine, I pressed the sub-basement button. I exited the elevator and immediately felt cold air. Next door to the elevator was a vintage winch. It looked sturdy enough, so I lowered myself through a bedrock shaft to the bottom of a wet, sandy-floored pit. I was in total darkness.

"As I fumbled for my flashlight, a voice ordered, 'No light.' I was instructed to remain in the dark until another person spoke to me. At this point, I explained why I had come and we made arrangements to barter oysters for clothing and candles. They also wanted sunglasses to shield their eyes from unwanted light. This went on for a long time. When the Morlocks heard the noisy hoist, they would know it was me.

"One day I arrived at the bottom of the pit, and there was no one to greet me. I turned on my flashlight and attempted to see where I was and get my bearings. I walked through a large drain dripping with sea water and when I turned a corner, I came eye to eye with a Morlock."

Rooster sipped some more coffee and seemed less nervous as he pressed on with his tale. "We were both surprised, as we almost walked into each other. We looked at each other for only seconds before the Morlock screeched in a high-pitched wail, covered his eyes from my flashlight, and wobbled off. Everyone believes this story so far, but it's what I tell next that nobody believes. The Morlock was completely bald and stood about four feet tall. His eyes were enormous, and I swear there were no eyelids. His ears were long and pointy, like an elf. He was bucktoothed and had elongated fingers and nails. He wore tattered clothing and when he ran, his gait was like that of an organ grinder's monkey."

Micko gave Rooster a slight nod indicating he believed him. Then he picked up the two empty coffee cups to refill them and wondered, *Is Rooster as fond of alcohol and drugs as the rest of the Mole People?*

The big chefs were gone and the nuns were cleaning up, so Micko knew they would be expelled soon. With fresh coffee, the two sat and discussed the Morlocks until they were asked to leave.

Micko spent the night in Joe's former residence, the red caboose. He thought about what he had learned about the Morlocks. He knew they were probably descendants from the first homeless moles two hundred years ago, similar to the vagrants and scavengers like today's underground communities, except over the centuries contractors built up cities above them.

How long were they living in total darkness with only candlelight? Could they have evolved into the beings Rooster described? If they lived in shallow tunnels, could that have a bearing on their stunted growth and uncanny waddle?

These and many other questions bothered Micko as he tried to sleep in the comfy caboose.

Micko rose early in the morning after a fitful sleep where he had visions of rat-faced troglodytes chasing him along gloomy train tunnels. He plugged in the coffee maker and plopped in a K-cup of Maxwell House. While the coffee brewed, he found some Pop Tarts and coffee creamers in the cooler chest, so he had a simple breakfast in the antique railroad car.

After his meal, Micko studied his maps and notes from the research material Joe Lombardi had given him and compared it to the schematics Esmeralda had sent. He was unsure if he should seek out the Phantom in the unchartered depths of the underworld labyrinth or if he should present himself to the various nomad communities. He decided to visit subterranean mayors with the hopes of ingratiating himself to them and possibly learning more on the location of his quarry.

Following his map and chalk-marking his way, Micko began the long walk from his caboose to the giant tunnel that housed The Hanoi Hilton. Along the way, he passed lengthy, well-lit, heated corridors with rows of insulated steam pipes. Then the map directed him through dark, clammy, narrow, concrete passageways. He stopped trying to figure out their purposes.

Suddenly a crack whore jumped out in front of him. "Got some, got some?" she begged as she held out her shaky hand.

Micko gave her a grief-stricken look and merely shook his head.

"I'll give you the best blow job you ever had mister," she pleaded.

The poor, disheveled girl was barely out of her teenage years and hopelessly lost. Still, a fix was the only thing on her mind.

"Why don't yer go 'um?" he muttered.

"And why don't you speak English, you Irish prick!" she screamed in return.

Micko continued on his way and never looked back at the wretched waif.

His map had him climb to upper levels through abandoned air shafts until he reached an operational subway tunnel. He checked his compass and took off in a northerly direction. Suddenly, the track lights switched from red to green, and Micko realized a subway train was approaching, but he didn't know from which direction.

Then, straight ahead, was the unmistakable brightness of an approaching train headlight rounding a turn. The light lit up the tunnel walls and Micko dashed into a doorway. The train zipped by noisily but harmlessly at about 20 mph. He was just glad it wasn't the Amtrak Acela Express train which traveled at

150 mph and speeds past you before you even hear it.

This was Micko's first encounter with live tracks or trains, and he knew he had better be vigilant while trekking through these subways. Esmeralda's research warned him about the dangers of walking along active train tracks. Unannounced changing of track switches, the electrified third rail, tunnel blackouts, and signal light changes all added to the threat.

Micko figured he had walked over a mile uptown in this twisting subway tunnel until the map directed him to open a utility room door. He recognized the door because it had a red X scrawled on it like Joe's map indicated.

Following the map, Micko climbed down a set of corroded ladder rungs that dived deep into the underbelly of the chasm. He finally landed in a cold, dimly lit catacomb of brick-covered alleys. There were six tunnels intersecting at this juncture. Each catacomb was lined with numerous water pipes, and Micko's compass was being affected by all the metal in his surroundings.

According to his chart, one of the catacombs should empty into a huge cinder-block-lined cave. Completely lost, Micko pulled up his collar to ward off the cold and grabbed his chalk. Climbing down the long shaft made him lose his sense of direction, so Micko picked the closest corridor and marked it with a big A and hiked in. After a few hundred yards, the base of the catacomb collected water and he thought he smelled salt water from the river.

Micko backtracked until he reached the intersection again. Now he knew which corridor went west, so it was easy to figure out which one went due north. He rubbed away the letter A and marked his new tunnel with a large N and ventured in. Soon this narrow passageway emptied into a mammoth room.

Micko knew this was the right place and made a few corrections on his map.

This gigantic tunnel was lined with massive slabs of concrete blocks. The engineering was flawless. Each seam between blocks was smooth and perfect. This tunnel was a testament to the skills of the masons and architects from a time when things were built to last.

Micko walked along this gigantic cave-like hallway that still bore a pair of ancient train tracks. He questioned if he was in the correct corridor and examined his map. He had stumbled upon a track juncture with an ancient switch housing that directed trains to move north or south.

When he put his chart away and took stock of his situation, he noticed two men in army fatigues walking his way. Micko raised his hands in a nonconfrontational manner and slowly walked to meet them.

"What took you so long?" one of the men asked.

Micko just shrugged his shoulders.

The two men studied him carefully, and when they were confident he posed no danger, they motioned him to follow. They walked north along the tunnel wall until a flickering fire was visible ahead.

A 55 gallon drum was a source of heat for a half dozen men in various tattered soldier uniforms. A man wearing a maroon, U.S. Army Airborne beret, asked, "The Nutty Irishman, I presume?"

Micko grunted and shook hands with the man. "I'm Quinn, the men call me The Mighty Quinn." Then he stepped up to the fire to warm his hands. Each man gave the other a quick once over.

Micko silently hoped Quinn saw a dirty, disheveled Nutty Irishman. Micko observed Quinn as a tall man with broad shoulders, lean face, and large hands. There was also a keen sense of authority and intelligence radiating from this man.

"Tom, Jerry, back on patrol until 1300 hours. You other guys hang loose while I give our new friend a tour of The Hanoi Hilton."

Micko raised his eyebrows to Quinn and he responded, "Yeah, their names really *are* Tom and Jerry."

Quinn smiled while Micko grinned.

They walked a hundred yards until they came upon an encampment. The first thing Micko noticed was an upside down American flag flying above a twelve-foot flagpole. This was the international symbol of distress. There was a colossal tent to the right of the tracks and an organized set of bivouacs to the left. The village resembled a military base camp. Each campsite was waterproofed and a thick wire cable ran from the ceiling high above.

Quinn looked up and said, "The Hudson Line railroad tracks run across our roof. They rudely allow their trains to shake our roof so badly that water and loose debris rain down on us from above. We thank the railroad by rudely tapping into their power supply."

The community was well lit and electric heaters and trash can fires kept the place warm. Ten yards away from the settlement, the chill was evident. Micko wondered where these people got all the wood to keep warm over all the years. Before he could ask Quinn, he quickly realized, *This is railroad country. Nothing but wooden railroad ties and metal tracks, you idiot.*

They walked under the enormous tent and it was like a huge cafeteria. A kitchen was set up with long rows of potbelly stoves and tables with accommodating benches. A sign read, *The Fly Farm.*

Several men and women were seated and lunching as they passed. Quinn led them past the mess hall into a large lounge area complete with a 65" television set, two pool tables, and a pair of card tables. Several couches and recliners concluded the setup.

Micko stared, disbelievingly, then look inquisitively at Quinn.

"I was told you don't speak much. We have been here a long time, and these things took a long time to come by. The television is only borrowed. The NYPD raided a numbers place and padlocked the joint. We unlocked it and borrowed a few leisurely items that you see here. Military personnel are great scroungers, and if you stay for dinner, you'll see how well we eat."

Micko pointed his shillelagh at the pristine bar.

"That was courtesy of a tenant landlord dispute. The Crown Lounge was run by a British gang. The landlord was Irish Paddy Doherty. Conflict was inevitable, and early one morning Paddy gave a few of our boys keys to the establishment. The rest is history." He smiled broadly.

Micko simply nodded his approval.

Quinn continued. "As you can see, we have all the creature comforts of you aboveground people."

"What aboyt de brutal apples?" Micko asked.

"Bad apples? Oh yeah, we have a few. Everyone here was military at one time or another so they know the rules. Drugs are not permitted. Drinking and smoking pot are permitted. If someone gets out of hand, my Outfit puts them in the stockade located at the other end of the encampment. If a soldier turns to drugs or is too mentally disabled to conform to our rules, then they are banished to Bungalow Town a half mile south of here. Only nonconformists live there. We have weeded out the unsuitable and now we have a fairly normal community. The lack of sufficient females is a problem, but we're working on it," Quinn added with a laugh.

A city beneath the rat race of Manhattan. Who would have known?

The Mighty Quinn was a gracious host and Micko thanked him heartily in his awful Irish accent. Micko expressed interest in visiting the Rotunda Kids, and Quinn pointed north and said, "Go straight, and then come back for dinner."

Just before he left Quinn, Micko asked, "Do yer nu wha Tiny is 'idin'?" Quinn didn't have much knowledge about his adversary, but said, "My Outfit and the vigilantes will get him for you . . . officer."

How did Quinn know? Did Joe Lombardi tell him? Was the Airborne Ranger that sharp? Would he tell the others?

The temperature dropped as Micko walked briskly to ward off the chill. He unexpectedly came across Bevo and Mango painting on the cave wall. After exchanging pleasant greetings, they proudly showed their newest creation.

It was an astonishingly accurate recreation of Hannity's Manor, with an oversized portrait of Hannity looking down from the sky in the upper left corner of the mural. The right corner of the landscape, away from the Renaissance Village, revealed a chilling depiction of Waste Way. Ghostly images rose from the shaft, while revolting skulls and bones littered the ground around the rim of the chute.

"We need a quotation from the Nutty Irishman to complete our creation," Bevo said.

Without hesitation, Micko slowly answered, "Will Bejasus ever forgive us for waaat we 'av done ter each other?"

Mango looked at Bevo and cried, "It's perfect!"

The pair of underground painters repeated the quote and worked on adding the phrase to their masterpiece.

Micko couldn't remember where he had heard that phrase. *In a church or movie?*

He left the busy artists and continued in the direction of the Rotunda. He wanted to make it back to the Hanoi Hilton for dinner.

He needed to know where he stood with the Mighty Quinn.

Tiny repeated his new routine of sharing breakfast with his ladies. While he sipped his coffee, he excitedly told them about his newfound water view. Although they could not answer him, Tiny had them placed where they faced him, as he spoke to them.

After breakfast, Tiny brushed their hair, applied perfume, and washed their exposed skin with olive oil. *If it was good enough for the Egyptians, it is good enough for my women. You can learn a lot from television.*

Tiny didn't think the women looked strange in their unusual rigor mortis poses, until his first victim's limbs became relaxed. He was washing his dishes after breakfast and found his first victim had fallen off the chair.

Tiny didn't understand the physics of rigor, and how it could come and go. When he picked her up and tried to replace her in the chair, her arms and legs were now rubbery. She no longer looked like a real woman, but a useless, lifeless ragdoll that would not sit upright.

This angered Tiny as he stared at this deformed lady. *Will this happen to the others?* It didn't take him too long to realize that as each woman became useless non-listeners, they needed to be replaced. Tiny organized the tools he would need for tonight's woman hunt.

Micko's trek through the colossal tunnel ended at a sharp drop where the towering ceiling was now a mere three feet high. It was like walking through a huge funnel that immediately narrowed and plunged deeper underground.

He knew he must be close to his destination with this radical change in geography as well as the salty smell of brine, indicating the closeness to the Hudson River.

This new passageway was dark and moist, so Micko rearranged his clothing for warmth and grabbed his flashlight. With his light in his left hand and his shillelagh in his right, he cautiously entered the lower corridor.

His flashlight must have given away his presence because he heard someone cry out, "Who's there?" Then there was an uproar from ahead.

Micko didn't answer but rounded a corner and came face to face with an old, rusty, metal gate. On the other side, candles glowed and moved about in a commotion.

A tall figure came to the gate carrying a lantern. "Ah, the Nutty Irishman. Welcome, welcome."

The man was in his early twenties and dark-skinned. He produced a key and opened the gate with a loud screech.

"We don't use this entrance often. Obviously, you visited The Hanoi Hilton first," he said.

The tall, dark man opened the noisy gate, stuck out his hand, and said, "Hello, my name is Ali."

Ali gave Micko a vigorous handshake and allowed him to pass through the gateway.

A small crowd had gathered as word spread that the Nutty Irishman was there. Some of the younger kids touched him and marveled at the beat-up shillelagh he carried.

Ali shooed them away and led Micko to an enormous, round-bricked cathedral. The room glowed with artificial light courtesy of contained fires, lanterns, and candles. Slabs were missing from various heights along the wall where lanterns and candles sat, giving off extra light. Large hollows were carved out of the walls to create safe havens for sleeping. The perimeter of the room was lined with sleeping bags, large boxes, shopping carts, and other items one associates with bag ladies. The interior of the cave was like a huge living room. Chairs, couches, and small tables were scattered about.

Ali gave Micko a quick rundown on the Rotunda. It was placed several stories underground, directly beneath a scenic topside rotunda. As others had already explained, access was difficult. The residents were considered losers by modern society. They consisted of petty criminals hiding from minor arrest warrants, drug addicts, sexual and physical abuse victims, and some just homeless for a wide variety of reasons.

Micko looked about the complex and Ali explained that the Rotunda Kids, depending on seniority, slept in or against the walls and gorges in fixed spots. The middle of the compound was for leisure activities—smoking, talking, eating, and just hanging out. Previous mayors allowed drinking and drugging in the compound, but Ali was the new mayor and enacted new laws prohibiting such activity. The complex rules discouraged drinking and drugging, but if a resident did get high outside the arena, they could still come back in. They just couldn't get high on the premises. Ali laughed that since he locked the secret grate entrance from above, it was too difficult to climb the twenty-five-foot fence while stoned.

Micko liked this kid. He was mature beyond his years and had a difficult job controlling rebellious teens. Keeping them safe was his main concern. Ali was smart and used every social service available to keep the residents healthy, well fed, and clothed.

"Come here. I want you to meet someone," Ali said. "This is Father Flynn from Our Lady of Lords Church. He is our liaison person with the outreach programs. He helps us with the soup kitchens, food and clothing drives, medical groups, and urgent care centers."

Micko immediately sized this man up as being a good servant of God. After exchanging a few courteous words, Father Flynn placed his arm around Micko's shoulder and said, "Come, walk with me."

Father Flynn explained the constant difficulties the Rotunda Kids faced daily . . . runaways as young as ten with nowhere to go, aimless and destined to die at a young age.

"You do know that we have members here who work in the bathhouses?" he asked.

Micko knew he must really look the part after letting his clothes get filthy and his beard and hair raggedy. He simply shrugged off the kindly offer. Then he got an idea. Before he had taken this assignment, he had read about a huge problem confronting the Catholic Church in Manhattan. Apparently, the negative press about an immoral priest's activities had caused a serious decline in church contributions. Not to mention the lawsuits, and parishioners pulling their children from the schools. In order to save money, the Archdiocese of New York was closing churches and schools in each of the five boroughs. Manhattan was losing two churches and three schools.

He looked Father Flynn in the eye and held his gaze throughout his presentation. Micko encouraged the good priest to consult with the Archbishop and make him an offer to turn the facilities slated for closure to be used to help the tremendous amount of homeless in NYC.

Micko watched the priest's reaction as he continued to explain that the positive press alone would be worth millions. Helping the homeless could remove the Roman Catholic Church's current black eye. There were enough structures being closed to selectively separate various homeless victims. Runaways and youths in one facility, veterans in another, and mental issues could be handled in yet another.

Father Flynn's eyes brightened then dimmed at the thought of giving relief to these needy unfortunates. "I can't possibly fight the Archdiocese on this," he said.

Micko's hazel eyes blazed as he raised his false Irish voice. "Did Thomas Edison girn dat it's too 'ard ter create light bulbs or de phonograph? Didn't yer man say, 'Our greatest weakness lies in givin' up? De most certain way ter succeed is alwus ter try jist wan more time?"

Now Father Flynn's eyes were radiant. "Yes, yes he did. This is a fight I will relish and make my greatest achievement!"

Micko sat on a chair facing Father Flynn and Ali, while they sat on a large couch. He turned the conversation to his search for Tiny.

Ali said, "The Rotunda Kids have no knowledge of him but we will keep our eyes and ears open."

Micko said, "I must go ter Hanoi Hilton. Me be invited fer dinner and wish ter learn more 'bout them."

Tiny was excited thinking about adding a new woman to his lifeless flock. The laws of rigor mortis baffled him. First the women were stiff and sat upright without a problem. Now, one by one, they went limp after a few days in the cooler. *Maybe I will lower the temperature and freeze the bodies to make them stiff again*, he thought.

At midnight, Tiny grabbed his tool bag and cargo bin and pushed his way to the platforms of the departing Long Island Rail Road trains. He had not taken a woman from here and hoped police presence would be lax.

With his pushcart hidden in a small darkened storage room at trackside, Tiny cautiously creeped along the train tracks to a hiding place. He was dismayed to see so many people crowding the terminal and decided to make himself comfortable and wait for the right moment.

Sitting under the outer lip of the platform afforded him concealment, yet he could see the commuters clearly. He was bursting with excitement as he witnessed many women dressed in red and wearing red scarves. There was a single police officer patrolling the platform, and Tiny wondered if he would get the opportunity to grab a straphanger tonight.

Soon, a train pulled in and a handful of passengers exited the cars and those waiting clambered aboard. Tiny hoped the train would depart and the officer would leave his post until the next train was due. Then he would grab the first red-scarfed woman that appeared for the next outgoing train.

Suddenly a small commotion erupted at the opposite end of the platform. Two intoxicated men argued and the police officer went in that direction to intervene. An older woman walking with a cane gave the drunks a wide berth as she carefully walked along the concrete path toward her train.

Unfortunately for her, the LIRR coach pulled out of the station as she ambled along the shadows of the platform.

Tiny struck quickly. He climbed behind a metal girder next to a railroad tool box. As soon as the elderly woman passed the tool shack, Tiny grabbed her and with his hand around her mouth he dragged her to the darkness of the tracks below. He used her red scarf to strangle the poor woman.

In minutes he had his new victim in the cart and was rolling her back to his fortress . . . Tiny's Place.

Micko left the Rotunda Kids and retraced his way back to the Hanoi Hilton. Just before he was in sight of the compound, he heard distinct banging on pipes. He figured scouts he couldn't see were informing the vets that a stranger approached. The distinctive lights from the village came into view and Quinn waited to greet him at the entrance. They gave each other a respectful nod and Quinn stated, "We have a special meal for you tonight. Large Marge is making her famous Hungarian stew."

Quinn led Micko to the Fly Farm tent, where a large gypsy woman surrounded by large pots handled a hefty ladle. She slopped the stew into bowls in the hands of the hungry men and women waiting in line. A huge basket at the end of the serving table contained stacks of homemade bread.

The pair took their place in line until it was their turn to be served. *Even the Mighty Quinn must wait in line.* Large Marge smiled at Micko as she plopped stew into his bowl, a smile pockmarked with broken and missing teeth. She also had the beginnings of a mustache that would make any young man jealous.

"Large Marge is also our resident fortune teller with a tent right next to the prison stockade. She is the one who advised me a police officer would be visiting the Hanoi Hilton. Her warning put me on guard, and I can usually spot a cop a mile away. You look too healthy to belong down here. You are too new and walk like military and are hunting for someone. Typical cop attitude. Don't worry, I won't blow your cover and will also help you find this Tiny or Phantom. The Nam vets don't normally send out vigilantes to find criminals because most of us are already criminals. We will do this to curry favor with our topside police," Quinn said.

Micko understood. His undercover act fooled the foolish but not the savvy like this Quinn. Dropping his terrible Irish brogue Micko asked, "Is there anything I can do for you when my quest is over?"

"Just leave us alone and forget where we live." He smiled warmly, and for the first time in a while Micko smiled back.

"This stew is really good, but I won't ask what kind of meat is in it," Micko said.

Quinn laughed. "No, you don't want to know."

Micko knew that almost any kind of meat can be tenderized, spiced up, and cooked to taste great.

The pair had a friendly conversation during dinner. Micko learned the Vietnam Vets had few visitors besides the runners and graffiti artists. Tom and Jerry left notes and a debit card behind a brick in a hidden section of a hallway. Runners checked the spot twice a week. If the note required supplies from above, the runner used the ATM card to take out the necessary cash. The runner generally got 10% as payment and dropped off the products to the Outfit. Some communities used hollow pipes to leave messages while others allowed runners free access to their villages, like Hannity's Manor.

The Mighty Quinn wisely had his vets collecting all they were owed by the government, so they lived comfortably and did not have to rely on illegal means to sustain themselves.

The Bungalow Town was the opposite and in disarray with the Section 8s selling drugs to support themselves. These vets ventured out of the depths of their fragile community to do business with the aboveground people. Violence was a daily part of their shortened lives. Besides drugging and living in squalor, these misfits had the morality of residents from Sodom and Gomorrah. Stabbings, crack whores, and all kinds of depravity defined the sordidness of this metropolis.

Micko learned a lot about subterranean life from Quinn. Bungalow Town seemed to be on the same depraved scale as Hannity's Shantytown. The completely unmanageable moles were expelled from the regular dysfunctional villages to live among other malcontents and incorrigibles. He thought, *How strange for one set of scalawags to pass judgment on other vagrants.*

Quinn must have really liked Micko because his honesty was refreshing. He begged the cop to forget about the Hanoi Hilton because many of the residents, although they were hiding from the law, had become model citizen moles. Hannity's Raiders routinely enter Bungalow Town to remove the dead. If Quinn had a death in the Hanoi Hilton, the runners notified Hannity so the corpse was removed before disease set in. The community mayors all agreed disease could wipe out the entire underground world very swiftly.

Micko realized as dysfunctional as the mole people were, they were somewhat organized. Even the insane could be reasonable at times. Although Micko was having a pleasant time with Quinn, the rest of the Vietnam Vets kept their distance.

These were older men, 65-75 years of age. They came to this place because they trusted no one but their own. To live underground and still be alive as seniors was amazing.

After dinner, Quinn introduced the Nutty Irishman to a group of vets watching television. They were disinterested and basically ignored him. When a commercial came on for Progressive motorcycle insurance, Micko got an idea.

"I once belonged ter de Bronx Chapter av de American Legion Riders an' we often ride wi' de Nam Knights. Any av yer guys ever ride wi' dem?"

Suddenly, ten pairs of eyes locked onto the Nutty Irishman and distrust was replaced with acceptance. No one there had ever ridden with the Nam Knights, but all were aware of them. This was the icebreaker he needed. Quinn brought beers all around and the group enjoyed a lively conversation.

Time underground was of no importance. There were no clocks or sun, and no one cared. People ate and slept when they felt like it. Most adhered to a semi-regular schedule since all had some sort of work duties but overall no strict time regulations.

Micko didn't want to check his vest watch, but he knew it was late. He tried to stifle a yawn but failed.

"Time for this one to go home," Quinn joked to the group.

Every member of the crowd shook hands with the Nutty Irishman and wished him well. Nobody asked him where he slept. The underground dwellers all had a similar creed that he saw scrawled upon a subway wall.

We leave our past, our failures, and our names aboveground.

CHAPTER
11

The walk back to his Penn Station secret hotel room was long and laborious. He finally got the hang of the underground neighborhoods and map use. Micko needed to get back to his room to check his phone for messages and give his verbal report to the chief of detectives.

Once he entered his room, he immediately opened the room safe containing his weapon, shield, wallet, and cell phone. Micko viewed several messages left on the phone and he spent the next hour answering them.

His first call was to Chief Clifford, and he updated him on his progress. Micko didn't tell the chief about the vigilante posse willing to help him capture the Phantom. *The less he knows of this the better.* Even though the chief allowed him to be unconventional in his thirst for a speedy arrest, this was a bit over the top.

Next Micko called Esmeralda, and they shared some intimate talk before he downloaded more diagrams of old Penn Station she had researched for him. It took another hour for the detective to put all the newly acquired schematics to paper so he could lock up his phone again.

The exhausted crime fighter lay on his comfortable hotel bed and in his mind reviewed his current state of affairs. He now knew that Tiny lived somewhere underground between Penn Station and Grand Central Station. Since tunnels ran at least ten stories underground, this was a lot of territory to cover. Fortunately runners were putting together a meeting with the secret societies of mayors to form a vigilante hunt for the Phantom.

Micko was trying to organize his next underground trip. In the morning, he would visit the Waldorf Astoria Gays and ask about Tiny. Afterward, he would travel below Grand Central Station and meet with Papa Miller and the Lost Souls.

At least he would have met with the various community mayors before the posse was formed. He already decided that asking the lower level Skell community for help would be counterproductive. Inviting the Morlocks for help was out of the question, yet he still wished to meet them and ask about Tiny.

The weary detective made some new notes to his maps and settled in for a good night's sleep.

Tiny pushed his new victim in his wheeled bin until he reached the sanctuary of Tiny's Place. He was overexcited with his new resident in tow. He carefully carried the old woman down to the walk-in refrigerator and laid her body on the bed. Her overcoat was spread over her head obscuring her features, so Tiny pulled the coat back.

He was immediately repulsed by the ghastly figure before him. The woman's face was crimson, her grotesquely swollen tongue had turned purplish and hung out of her mouth.

He realized what had happened. The previous victims' necks were snapped. This woman he eagerly strangled with the notorious red scarf causing this distorted facial bloating.

Looking at this woman in contempt, he knew neck shattering was the only way to kill his victims if he were to keep them looking somewhat normal. Tiny picked up the corpse and hung it on one of the livestock meat hooks in the rear of the freezer. He didn't want to see it anymore.

Although this new victim was useless to him, he still got excited by the kill. He had a pressing need to both kill again and add to his dead women's society. Tiny eagerly awaited the night so he could prowl the late-night platforms looking for another victim.

Captain Pedone paced his office like a caged animal. He had just fielded two phone calls from families inquiring about loved ones. Both women had come to Manhattan by train to Penn Station but never returned home.

Since the complainants could not place Penn Station as the source of their loved ones going missing, the captain advised the callers to phone local hospitals and police stations in an effort to locate the lost. They insisted that the Phantom of Penn Station had them.

"The local NYPD precincts handle missing persons in Manhattan," he advised the callers. Still, he knew. The two women were scheduled to return home via trains from Penn Station.

His pacing continued as he thought about his next course of action. The task force would take this new information lightly, and his supervisors would dismiss it outright. This close to Christmas, everyone wished a trouble-free holiday season.

Pedone knew he had a kidnapping problem. Without ransom notes, he was sure the missings were dead. A serial killer was seeking shelter under his nose in the labyrinth below Penn Station.

His next phone call was to alert Micko of this new distressing information.

"Micko, when you get this recording call me back forthwith. We have a big problem. A really big problem. I think the Phantom is real."

While Captain Pedone was leaving a disturbing phone message on Micko's locked-up phone, the detective was having breakfast in Dunkin' Donuts. He hated coming here after seeing the homeless sleeping in the alley behind the premises, but he was hungry and there was no food in his room.

"Now I remember you," spoke a smiling Popeye.

Micko looked up from his jelly donut and coffee. "Good morning, Slugger."

"Still eating cop food I see," he said.

"Once a cop, always a cop."

Micko was glad to see that Slugger O'Toole had not started drinking this early and was still lucid. "How about a cup of coffee?" he asked.

"Naw, my stomach is acting up on me. It's the only time I'm off the sauce."

Micko and Popeye enjoyed a decent conversation while commuters raced about the station like a horde of whirling dervishes. The undercover cop explained his plight to the ex-boxer. They both kicked around a few ideas.

Popeye asked, "Why don't you use the keys that Captain Pedone gave you to gain easier access to the lower levels instead of climbing up and down dangerous staircases?"

"I'm not really sure what they open," he answered.

"The keys should give you access to the freight elevator that stops all the way down to the bedrock. It's the elevator behind the Amtrak loading dock," Popeye said.

Micko remembered this elevator from the last time he had worked in Penn Station. The elevator used to restock the Amtrak cafeteria cars only went down three floors. This hidden, unused, freight elevator was scary. It went all the way down to the lowest level. It rode down next to the ancient airshafts.

Pedone had given him this elevator key on the same key ring as the secret apartment and machinery room. He had forgotten the significance of this key.

"Popeye, you're a genius!" Micko said.

"No, I'm punch drunk but still smarter than a cop."

The two laughed and when Micko finished his last sip of coffee, he walked Popeye to the nearest variety store and bought a bottle of Pepto Bismol. "Drink it in good health."

"And you be careful with the Mole People," Popeye warned.

Micko made his way to the hidden freight elevator behind the loading dock. There was a lot of activity at this hour, so the undercover cop had to sneak around until he was sure he could take the lift down undetected.

He used the key to open the outer gate to the elevator. Then he pulled open the inner gate, allowing access to the lift's door. Once inside he pressed the down button for the fourth sublevel floor. The elevator creaked and groaned as it strained on its antique pulleys and gears.

It was a scary ride down in an elevator that screeched and vibrated. When it stopped, Micko consulted his map to see which level would take him to the abandoned Waldorf Astoria Hotel. The map indicated sublevel six would leave him in a desolate, crosstown railroad tunnel running all the way to Second Avenue on the east side.

Micko took the noisy craft down two more levels and exited to a dingy platform. It was so cold and damp, he could see his breath in the cool air.

He buttoned up his clothing, wielded his shillelagh, and grasped the flashlight. Micko knew it would be a long walk, and he may run into an assortment of lower-level Skells along the way. These nomads had no community ties and lived life on the very edge. People like this were the most dangerous.

The freight lines archway tunnel stretched wide with a high roof. Numerous ancient wires dangled, like dead tentacles from a prehistoric creature. The bricks were a dull gray color but expertly laid in smooth detail along the walls.

The chilled cop walked east at a brisk pace to warm up in the shadowy catacombs along the uninhibited tracks. With the exception of track rabbits, no sign of life was visible. Some of the passageway was faintly lit, but every once in a while the tunnel went dark for hundreds of yards. This was when Micko felt the most nervous.

Fear of the dark has always been one of mankind's most dreaded terrors.

Even when standing still, Micko heard strange, unseen noises.

What was that? A rat? Escaping steam from another corridor? A Skell waiting to disembowel me? A Morlock? No, please, not a Morlock.

His mind played bizarre games in the pitch black when alone.

I should have taken my gun and phone with me. No, can't do that. I should have taken the subway shuttle from Penn Station to Grand Central and worked my way to the lower levels. No, I must look for Tiny along these long, narrow tunnels.

Even with the powerful flashlight, the fear was still there.

Am I advertising my presence to unknown enemies? What is that noise!

Micko heard his heart beating inside his chest and sweat beaded on his brow.

He stopped and took a deep breath. Micko decided he would walk along the wall on the right side of the tracks rather than down the middle. This way he could have time to fend off an attack from the left and hopefully be aware of one from in front.

After what seemed like hours, the tunnel became brighter. The sweating stopped and his breathing returned to normal. The tunnel ran long and straight.

Eventually Micko came upon an abandoned Fifth Avenue subway station. The area was still somewhat well-lit, dry, and clean. He sat and removed his knapsack so he could have a drink of water and peruse his map. The colorful wall tiles were graffiti-free and looked like they had been cleaned recently. But he knew that was not possible.

He was close to Grand Central Station but even closer to Track 61, which allowed access to the now defunct Waldorf Astoria Hotel. Micko looked through his knapsack and pulled out a Slim Jim sausage treat to go along with the water. While snacking, he took out his web downloads on the Waldorf.

The Waldorf Astoria Hotel was built in 1913 by the wealthy Vanderbilt family. It covered an entire city block from Park Avenue to Lexington Avenue and 49th Street to 50th Street. There were many secrets surrounding this lavish hotel.

Special rooms, elevators, suites, and private dining rooms were strategically placed. There was a private garage for dignitaries and even a special train track and platform. This was known as Track 61. The rich and famous took their private subway train to Track 61 and entered a distinct elevator leading to a secret garage. From there they would take another special elevator to their private rooms.

It was reported that after suffering a heart attack, General John J. Pershing was the first to take a private train along Track 61 and use the ultra-secret entrance to the extravagant hotel. The most famous visitor was President Franklin D. Roosevelt, who did not want the public to see he was a paraplegic from having contracted polio at age thirty-nine.

The Waldorf Astoria Hotel covered forty-nine square acres of land when it was built. Now that time had built above the archaic hotel, there were forty-nine acres of Waldorf Astoria Hotel several levels underground.

The special train that President Roosevelt used still sat on Track 61. In better times, tours were allowed to view this unusual railroad car. In the 1960s, Track 61 fell into a serious state of disrepair and homeless squatters took up residence in the area. It has been rumored that Andy Warhol once hosted an underground party in the historic rail car.

Most people did not realize today's Grand Central Station and Waldorf Astoria Hotel were built over the earlier versions resting deep underground. Micko continued to read the fascinating history of this area and learned the current topside Waldorf was closed for a three-year major restoration period.

Micko packed up his bag and continued on his journey. He kept his map handy since he had to locate the hidden track-rerouting switch to divert a train off this main path and onto Track 61.

Ten minutes later, he discovered the redirecting station. He didn't really need a map to locate it. A dirty tunnel forked from the main line with the track switch being protected by a threatening housing cover painted with: *Danger. High Voltage. Do Not Touch.*

It would not be easy for anyone to switch a train to Track 61. Micko was appalled by the squalor of this new train line compared to the relatively pristine one he walked.

The walls were caked with so much brown gunk he couldn't tell what the natural color had been. A brownish film covered everything including the rusty train rails. It looked like heavy, brown dust. Old newspapers and trash covered the entire area. Repulsive graffiti stained huge sections of the cement walls. *I should get Bevo and Mango to come down here and add some nice art to these halls*, he thought.

Micko had seen a lot of subterranean areas since he began this assignment. Most were cold and damp, some even wet, but this was filthy.

After about 100 yards, the tracks and tunnel suddenly took a sharp right turn and entered the secret station below the Waldorf. The transformation was mesmerizing. Suddenly, the track area was miraculously clean. The tunnel walls were freshly painted in psychedelic colors reminding the cop of Jimi Hendrix's song, "Purple Haze."

The dilapidated train car that once belonged to President Roosevelt sat coupled to two freshly painted coach cars that looked like a 1960s hippie van. Peace signs and love symbols adorned the colorful carriages.

Micko was shocked by the transformation that was more stunning than a caterpillar to butterfly. He had just walked through Hades to enter Woodstock.

A loud voice bellowed, "Hey man, what do you want?"

Micko turned his gaze from the kaleidoscopic train cars and glimpsed a large, muscular man dressed in leather gear.

"I'm de Nutty Oirishman," Micko said.

The leather-clad dude looked him over carefully before motioning him toward the hidden elevator. The buttons on the lift's walls indicated four floors, but the dude took him to floor number two.

When the elevator doors squeaked opened, Micko got the second OMG moment of the day. He stepped into an act right out of the dance scene from *Saturday Night Fever*.

A huge silver disco ball hung from above as dozens of people dressed in '70s style clothing danced to an ABBA song. Most of the dancers looked gay. Some dressed as women, others as men, but their over exaggerated girlish gait was evident. Others appeared to be rich, straight patrons who enjoyed the gay scene.

The predominant color was pink. Pink walls. Pink tables and chairs. Pink boas adorned the necks of female-dressed dancers. A huge bar rested against the far wall, made entirely of glass. Twenty or thirty people sat or stood at the bar. Their attire was laughable, like most gay club regulars are to straight people.

"Jimmy Joe is in there," Mr. Muscles pointed to a pastel blue door to the left.

Micko crossed the dance floor to reach the desired door and was abused by a number of cat calls, whistles, and derogatory remarks regarding his attire.

After two hard knocks, a voice answered immediately. "Come in."

Micko marched in, head up high, and before he could announce himself, his host calmly said, "Sit down, Irish, I'm Jimmy Joe."

The undercover cop quickly sized up his host as he sat in a plush, black leather recliner. Jimmy Joe spoke with a southern drawl, was dressed in an expensive business suit, and A. Testoni shoes.

He looked like a Wall Street broker sitting behind a massive, black executive desk. A box of Cohiba Behike cigars perched on the right side of the desk and a carafe of red wine sat nestled in the left corner.

Jimmy Joe, noticing the Nutty Irishman's internal observations, said, "I ran a gay nightclub in Atlanta, Georgia. I had a successful business until the local politicians passed a new ordinance prohibiting my club from operating within certain city limits.

"Without warning, local police officers ransacked the discotheque and drove me out of town with a stern warning. Don't come back!

"I decided to try my hand at a gay club in Manhattan. While seeking business partners in the Meat Packing District, I was severely beaten by a group of bikers. Some homeless gays dragged me underground and tended to my wounds. Months later, my rescuers introduced me to the mayor of the Waldorf Astoria Gays, Weird Waldo."

He explained how the Waldorf Gays lived in obscene conditions until he organized a huge cleanup rally that attracted a colossal number of volunteers. The cleanup took six months, and little by little, they renovated the empty station to modernize the shabby club. Jimmy Joe was the actual person who knocked down several walls to discover the deserted hotel rooms that they turned into the current nightclub.

Another six months of cleanups and the disco was open for business, Weird Waldo passed away, and Jimmy Joe became the new mayor. That was three years ago, and the club was still thriving 24/7. The other hotel rooms were cleaned up and became living quarters for the gay staff members and wealthy visitors. Rooms couldn't be renovated above the fourth floor because it was not architecturally safe.

Micko was again overwhelmed and opened his arms at the opulence of Jimmy Joe's office.

The gracious host continued his tale of perseverance and hard work. The lavishness of his office was his reward and sanctuary. He was a very capable manager of the discotheque he called the Barracuda Lounge, and an assortment of people frequented the establishment.

"You would not believe how many actors and actresses have visited. Even some noted sports stars have danced and drunk here. It seems the more outrageous a place is, the more popular it becomes. We have entertained people that are AC, DC, or no current at all," he said.

"My leather-clad band of Rowdies cleared the homeless from not only this small section of Track 61 but from the entire tunnel from the west side to the east side."

Now Micko knew why he had never encountered a Skell along the way. Jimmy Joe's Rowdies chased them away. If the other Rowdies were built like Mr. Muscles, it's no wonder the Skells stayed away.

"My Rowdies have been following you since you entered the vacant tunnel. They know who you are and sent a runner to alert me. Please stay and have a drink. You look like a beer man to me," he said, as he looked at his guest's mini beer belly.

Micko grinned and shook his head in the affirmative as Jimmy Joe opened a small refrigerator. His host pulled out a bottle of Becks and a bottle of Stella. Micko pointed to the Becks.

While Jimmy Joe poured beer into a glass, Micko continued to investigate the other parts of the office. It was obvious Jimmy Joe was a collector of a wide variety of mantle clocks. He had shelves along the walls adorned with exquisite desk clocks. The dark wood-paneled walls coordinated with the dark wood of his desk. Everything in the room matched.

Jimmy Joe handed the Nutty Irishman his beer and poured himself a small glass of wine from the decanter on his desk. They raised their glasses to each other in silence and took a sip. Jimmy Joe continued.

"The club does well money-wise, so the homeless are well taken care of. They don't want for anything as long as they continue to work hard and behave. The disco has parties day and night, so the Waldorf Gays have to be sober and sane. The ones who cannot conform are sent back above to languish in the streets as homeless refuges from the Barracuda Lounge. The Rowdies keep the peace down here. Expensive private parties are held in the downstairs nightclub called the Wail Way. Exploring FDR's antique rail car is a draw, but not nearly as popular as the hippie-painted bar car and the attached rumpus room coach. The noise that emanates from the sex room car is what gives the trackside nightclub its strange name."

He explained about the many types of people who patronized both the Wail Way nightclub and the Barracuda Lounge.

"Some are simple daffodils who drink cosmopolitans. The muscle-bound biker types prefer gin and tonic. There are a long list of other types including the sexually adventurous or gender confused. There is never a dull moment down here," he said, with mockery in his voice.

Micko drank a long draught from his beer and thought, *What a great idea. Training the homeless to seduce the upper crust with sex, alcohol, and a hippie whorehouse train.*

Amazingly, the two completely opposite men got along well. Micko spoke more to this mayor than all the others combined. Neither man judged the other. They just spoke frankly about underground life in the straight and gay communities.

Undesirables left these people alone and preyed on others. The seedy allure and pretty lounges were compelling attractions to both straights and gays alike.

"We have many theme nights in the Barracuda Lounge: oldies night, wicked costume night, outrageous shirt night, crazy hat night, and many other crowd pleasers. The theme parties are advertised in a special coded section of the *Village Voice* newspaper. Interested parties take a train to the 51st Street Station and meet a guide who leads them down an old spiral staircase, across a catwalk to a hidden fire escape, and down to Track 61. This leads to a short walk along the seedier part of the track to the platform. This forbidding path is a great allure for the fans," he said.

During their animated conversation, Micko asked about Tiny. Jimmy Joe said he only heard of him when his daily runners had mentioned him. Apparently Tiny had never been to the eastern section of the netherworld.

Micko thanked his host for the beer and hospitality and said he would continue east to Grand Central Station.

"Be very careful. You have your No Zone on the west side and 100 yards east is our No Zone. Many Skells are known to frequent this No Zone," Jimmy Joe warned.

Mr. Muscles led Micko back the way they had come. When Micko headed east and waved back at Mr. Muscles, the man just shook his head in hopelessness for the Nutty Irishman's expedition.

CHAPTER

12

Tiny was very disappointed in his latest kidnapping. The old woman's face continued to haunt him. He knew he must add to his current flock and do it quickly. His urges had increased again.

Tonight, he would stealthily cruise the Amtrak uptown train platforms until he located a young woman dressed in a red scarf. He realized he might have to sit in the darkness and wait hours until he could strike, but this only aroused him more.

Krissy clocked out from her job as a cashier at Amir's Falafel Hut at 8:00 p.m. She quickly walked the short distance to meet her boyfriend, Frankie, in front of Madison Square Garden.

She jumped up and gave him a big kiss, then asked, "Do you have it?" When Frankie nodded with a smile, she hugged him and grabbed his hand and led him down the street and into Penn Station.

Soon the pair was sitting under the platform to Track 9. Frankie was a huge Roger Maris fan, so they always got high under Track 9 since nine was the jersey number Maris wore when he played for the NY Yankees in the 1960s.

Frankie cooked his heroin and carefully loaded it into his syringe as Krissy watched. Soon after injecting the heroin, with the street name Tango & Cash, Frankie's eyes rolled back into his head and he drifted off into a drowsy euphoria.

Krissy made sure Frankie was comfortable before she snorted her dose of heroin laced with fentanyl. She had a fear of needles but still loved the magnificent high she got from the opioids. She made sure she had naloxone in her pocket in case Frankie overdosed. She mistakenly thought only mainliners could OD.

It didn't take long before Krissy joined Frankie in the enraptured magical mystery tour of drug-induced slumber. Sadly, their entire lives revolved around this addicted moment.

Micko walked east along the deserted railroad tracks until they suddenly took a sharp turn left and merged with the original East/West Tunnel.

Windblown newspapers and other litter flew through the unlit tunnel as Micko walked eastbound. The walls were covered in spray-painted graffiti and tag lines with STP13 being the most prolific. Unlike the beautiful murals painted by Bevo and Mango, these were ghetto marks by uninspired and untalented taggers.

This eastern section of the netherworld had a different, darker complexion than the west side. Soon Micko came upon numerous hovels of homeless littering the shadowy edges of the track corridors. Sleeping bags, stuffed shopping carts, and empty boxes littered the area.

Micko felt hidden eyes following his every move. Suddenly, a homeless nomad with a single crutch lurched at him from out of the blackness.

The demented man screamed obscenities at Micko as he waved his crutch in a menacing manner. The undercover cop, startled, backed up from the lunatic.

The Skell grabbed his crutch in both hands like a baseball bat and swung it at Micko. Luckily, the crutch swung back and forth several feet from him, but between swings, Micko used his shillelagh to smack the bum on the left side of his head.

The man went down hard and sprawled across the train tracks. Micko was afraid he hit the Mole Man too hard and reached down to help him to his feet.

The derelict was fast. He drew a 6" steak knife from inside the rubber crutch cushion and sliced it through Micko's coat sleeve right down to his skin.

Micko pulled back, grabbing his bleeding forearm as the beggar soundlessly ran back into the safety of the trackside shadows.

He shined his flashlight onto the wound but couldn't tell how bad it was. Micko wrapped his handkerchief around the cut and decided it was better to be safe than sorry. He thought it best to seek medical treatment at Hannity's Manor from Nurse Cotton Top rather than seek out Papa Miller and the Lost Souls.

Micko pulled out his map and constructed his quickest way back to Hannity's hospital tent. He climbed several levels and took the 42nd Street crosstown subway train shuttle back to Penn Station, then down several levels to Hannity's Manor.

Captain Pedone was angry. The random kidnappings had gotten out of control. Even though he wanted to handle things the correct way right from the start, he was now being blamed by the same people that obstructed him since the beginning.

The family of the first missing woman went to the local newspaper to complain about the lack of cooperation from the Amtrak Police. When a certain crime reporter learned several women had gone missing from Penn Station, he rewrote his earlier shocking story about the Phantom of Penn Station, who was kidnapping women for mysterious reasons yet to be determined. The other media outlets loved the idea of the Phantom of Penn Station, so they also ran with it. This put huge pressure on Penn Station and police officials.

The Amtrak hierarchy, the FBI, and the general public all wanted his head. Pedone had asked to take constructive action earlier, but his bosses denied his requests. Now, he was being blamed.

The hapless captain left several messages on Micko's phone, knowing the phone was probably locked up in the hotel room safe. He had no idea when the undercover cop would retrieve the messages.

His own phone rang constantly as everyone demanded the Phantom be arrested immediately and the kidnapped women be released ASAP.

Tiny was on the hunt for a new, younger woman. He pushed his cargo bin along filthy corridors and alleys until he reached the shadows leading to the Amtrak platforms. He hid the cart in the darkness and quietly edged closer to the wooden train track podium.

He silently slipped under the platform and waited until his eyes adjusted to the new darkness. He would sit there until the next train left the station and would abduct a lone traveler waiting for the following train.

Krissy stirred as the euphoric effects of her drugs wore off. She sat up in the darkness, slowly letting her eyes adjust. When her eyes cleared, she looked about for Frankie. He was gone. He must have woken up earlier and was out trying to score another fix.

She heard a noise under the platform. "Is that you, Frankie?" she whispered.

Suddenly, she spotted a huge, dark figure with great white eyes reach out for her. A giant ham hock hand closed around her mouth, stifling her scream. The hand covered her mouth and nose, and she slipped into unconsciousness.

Tiny was as surprised as the woman. He knew junkies often did drugs under the train platforms but hadn't seen her until she stirred and cried out. Now he took a closer look at this new victim. She was a young, white girl wearing a puffy blue ski coat, a red wool cap, and matching red scarf.

Perfect, he thought, as he removed her from the confines of the tight space and placed her in the cart. Half an hour later, his new lady was lying on the bed in the refrigerator dorm room. The other ladies were sitting at the small table. He would have to clean up this new lady before she joined the others.

Tiny was pleased with himself and felt a warm tingling sensation. He liked his women but also liked the feeling of dominance by killing at will. This was his new passion in life—taking other lives. By suffocating this victim rather than strangling, the face was not distorted. He also hoped her head would sit straight upon her shoulders rather than dangle like the ones with the broken necks.

He went into the kitchen area to cook up a congratulatory meal for himself, before talking to his ladies about his latest conquest. Tiny turned on the CD player and blasted rap music loudly as he cooked and pranced about in the galley. He would have a nice meal before cleaning his new lady.

Soon he had his New England clam chowder and grilled cheese sandwich ready and placed on a carry tray. Tiny walked triumphantly down the basement into the refrigerator room and sat with his ladies. He consumed the meal and bragged about how stealthily he had seized his new victim.

Tiny pointed toward the bed and told his sitting ladies, "Soon I will clean her, and she will join us here at . . ."

His sentence trailed off as he realized his new conquest was gone. Tiny jumped up from the chair so fast, he knocked over his meal, the small table, and the ladies seated at it.

He ran toward the bed to see if she had rolled off and out of sight. No. She was gone. He now realized that in his haste to keep the woman quiet and remove her from the confines of the tracks, he only smothered her to unconsciousness, not death.

Tiny was confused. Where could she have gone? The front door was padlocked, and there were no other unlocked exits.

He quickly searched the entire restaurant. He thought she left the refrigerator while he was cooking, but she was nowhere to be found. He checked his living quarters, the eating area, the bathroom, and even storage rooms and cabinets.

Sullenly, he retreated back to his refrigerated dorm to reseat the ladies and their table. While he picked up the remnants of the meal from the floor, he glimpsed a light coming from under a door at the rear of the room.

Tiny opened the door. It was the compressor room for the freezer. A small vent screen was missing. Looking out the portal, he saw it led to a rubbish-filled alley behind the café. She was alive . . . and gone. She would warn others. His refuge was compromised. To elude the police, Tiny must find a new subterranean home. He quickly packed his bags to begin searching the netherworld for a new haven.

Worst of all, he had to leave his ladies behind.

Krissy coughed and spit up blood. The giant's hand had caused her a nosebleed. She sat up on the bed dazed, but the cold air revived her. Krissy looked about her surroundings and realized she was in a large walk-in freezer.

Three women sat silently at a small table. Loud music blared from outside the freezer. Krissy called out lightly to the women who had their backs to her. No response, so she tried again, louder this time.

Frustrated, Krissy walked up to them and demanded to know where they were and why they wouldn't answer her. As Krissy got closer, the answer became evident. The women had icicles forming around their noses, ears, and mouths. The eyes had sunk into the cavities behind their faces, and they were posed like mannequins.

Krissy put her hand over her mouth to stifle a terrifying

scream as she realized the horror before her. She bravely opened the freezer door and looked out. She heard someone cooking in a kitchen with music booming.

She stepped up the stairs to the café lobby to the padlock and deadbolt on the front door. All of the windows were boarded up long ago as were all the exit doors.

Krissy walked back down into the freezer and headed toward the rear. She nearly screamed out loud when she saw the old lady dangling lifeless from the overhead hook.

She opened the door in the rear corner and turned on the light switch. She immediately recognized the chamber as a compressor room with a tool box on the floor.

Krissy withdrew a screwdriver from the tool box and pried off a small vent cover. Luckily she was slender enough to climb through the vent and exit into the outer alley. She ran like her life depended on it . . . because it did.

Micko rode the shuttle train from Grand Central Station to Penn Station. The ride was short and uneventful as he rode with his injured arm elevated so blood would not drip out of his sleeve.

The shuttle train was packed and the straphangers looked at him in utter disgust. He was the recipient of the hatred and prejudices that the homeless endured.

When he arrived at Penn Station, Micko walked quickly in the middle of the chaotic rush of holiday shoppers. Nobody saw his injury except Popeye.

"What's wrong, detective?" he asked.

Micko was surprised he was recognized in the crowd.

"What makes you think I'm injured?" he asked.

"Because you look like Napoléon Bonaparte with your arm stuck in your coat that way," Popeye answered.

Micko was surprised to see Popeye sober. "Is your stomach still bothering you?" he asked.

"It's killing me. I can't even hold down coffee anymore," he replied.

"Come with me. I'm headed for the infirmary at Hannity's Manor. They might have something to help you."

The two walked to a special alley and took a secret stairway two floors lower to a derelict subway station. From there they entered a noisy underground corridor. The hallway was a conduit of water pipes that clanged incessantly.

The banging ceased just before the duo exited the chamber and entered the cave structure leading to Hannity and his Rats. Quickly, they were met by several of Hannity's centurions. The guardians knew both Popeye and the Nutty Irishman, so they were led through the Renaissance Village to the Manor.

A smiling Hannity inquired, "To what do I owe this pleasure?"

Returning to undercover mode, the Nutty Irishman pulled back his coat sleeve to reveal the ugly wound. Popeye rubbed his stomach.

Hannity understood and led them to the hospital tent. Once inside, Cotton Top looked up from a patient. She was surprised to see the two visitors. The caring nurse reassured the pregnant patient she would return shortly.

The Nutty Irishman took off his coat and sweater to reveal his wound. Cotton Top looked at it and poured some hydrogen peroxide on the cut.

"This will require a few stitches," she said as she looked the Nutty Irishman in the eye.

"How aboyt jist usin' sum butterfly stitches?" he answered.

"I'll try, but if they don't stop the bleeding, you will need sutures."

Delicately, and professionally, Cotton Top applied antibiotic ointment and sterile adhesive skin closure strips to the laceration. It appeared to be working as the bleeding subsided. She then wrapped a piece of gauze around the gash and taped it up.

"You should get a tetanus shot at a topside clinic. If the wound swells and the bandaging gets too tight, you will have to come back," Cotton Top advised.

"You did a grn' job, an' oi tanks. Me mucker 'ere is a 'eavy drinker who is sufferin' from gut aches. Can yer 'elp 'imself?"

Popeye was comically shy in front of this adept nurse. Cotton Top was attractive, well-groomed, and displayed good leadership skills. These traits appeared to intimidate the sickly pugilist, and he was mesmerized by her cotton-white hair.

"I've seen a lot of this since I joined Hannity's hospital," she said.

The nurse led her patient to another room as the Nutty Irishman rejoined Hannity.

"We are having trouble arranging a meeting with all the mayors. Each society wants the meeting on their turf. In the past, our meetings were held here because of the easy access points. These days, there are new mayors and different viewpoints. The runners are acting as liaisons but are getting nowhere fast," Hannity said.

"This meetin' an' de capture av Tiny is critical," said the Nutty Irishman.

"Haven't you seen the newspapers? They are calling Tiny the Phantom of Penn Station. They say he is kidnapping women and hiding them down here in subterranean lairs," Hannity said. "So, which one of them belongs to you?"

The Nutty Irishman just waved his hand in disgust. The mayors believed the Phantom took something from him. The newspapers had gotten into the act. This might blow his cover. He might have to pretend a close relative is one of the missing.

He related this updated version of his quest for Tiny to Hannity and the reason why they had to act fast. If the mayor of NYC sent a search party underground, all the secret societies would be in danger. They had to find a neutral spot for the meeting. He suggested Shantytown and then no mayor would take credit.

Hannity liked this idea. If the Phantom wasn't caught quickly, the entire underground civilization was doomed. He sent his Raiders out to look for Rooster and any other runner they could find. They had to flush out this interloper.

Popeye rejoined his pal and showed him a large bottle of medicine.

"I took one gulp, and I already feel good. I also have these Antabuse pills to help me stay off the sauce until my stomach settles down. Hey, maybe I'll go on the wagon for good," he said.

The Nutty Irishman slapped his buddy on the back as he laughed out loud. The two headed back to the Penn Station waiting room. Popeye walked back to his begging spot and the Nutty Irishman decided to buy a coffee and bring it back to his secret hotel room.

CHAPTER
13

Krissy ran like a deer until she was completely exhausted. She had no idea where she was. She ran through dimly lit corridors and darkened alleys. She tripped several times over unseen objects, and her knees and elbows were badly scraped.

While trying to catch her breath and shake off the effects of her opioids, Krissy sobbed. She knew the other women were dead, and she almost joined them in their lifeless netherworld.

Eventually, Krissy became composed and took stock of her plight. She couldn't walk around crying out for help for fear the giant might hear her and catch her again. She was completely out of her element and didn't know where to go. She was in a poorly lit area of the underground, and she didn't have a flashlight.

She pulled a cigarette lighter from her pocket, the same lighter used to help Frankie cook his dope. Krissy shined the open flame near the ground until she found some old discarded boxes. She ripped them up and jerry-rigged a torch.

Krissy slowly walked along archaic railroad tracks looking for an outlet leading to civilization, when suddenly someone yelled, "Put that flame out before you start a fire!"

Frozen with fear, Krissy stood motionless, like a statue. A short black youth walked up to her, gently took the burning cardboard from her hand, and stomped the fire out.

"My name is Rooster. What are you doing here?" he asked.

She recognized Rooster as a regular at Penn Station and was relieved to see him.

"My name is Krissy, and I was under a platform with my boyfriend. We fell asleep, but when I woke up he was gone and a giant of a man smothered me into unconsciousness. I woke up in the freezer of a boarded-up restaurant and saw three other women. They were dead and propped up like dolls sitting at a small table. I escaped and now you found me."

Roosted shined his lantern up and down her profile and saw the ripped knees of her dungarees and the cuts on her limbs. "Come with me. I'll take you somewhere safe."

Micko picked up a discarded newspaper from an empty table in Dunkin' Donuts. With coffee and paper, he walked to his hidden room. Once inside he read about the Phantom of Penn Station as he sipped on his brew.

He knew this was real bad. The media thrived on sensationalism and this story *was* sensational. The previous posting of this story was lame, but now it was energized. Man's worst

primal fears were exposed as stories of kidnappings and prisoners hidden in dark underground dungeons overwhelmed all
the news outlets. Men, women, and children were horrified at
the constant news media coverage of the Phantom.

The people of New York demanded action from the mayor,
the NYPD, and the Amtrak PD. Micko knew he had only a
day or two to wrap this case up before it became a debacle.

Micko retrieved his cell phone from the safe and heard the
panicked messages left by Pedone and Clifford. He decided to
phone Chief Clifford first.

"Micko, this has gotten way out of hand since the news
media got involved. Tomorrow I have a meeting with the
mayor and the director of the New York branch of the FBI."

"Chief, I have made great progress, but I need a little more
time. I have underground dwellers and squatters looking for
the Phantom. I believe they can flush him out, if not outright capture the maniac. If the mayor decides to flood the
underground tunnels with police, I fear a subterranean war
will erupt," Micko replied.

"You are out of time. I am out of time. Whatever plan the
mayor and FBI decide on will be executed immediately. It
probably will include saturating police into the lower levels of
Penn Station to look for the victims and the Phantom."

The two ran several ideas back and forth, but they knew
delay tactics would not be viable. The entire country, if not the
world, was watching this scenario play out in Manhattan just
before Christmas.

Micko called Captain Pedone next and had a similar conversation. Pedone did offer an explanation to why a large
number of law enforcement officers could not engulf the
underground. "With extra trains running in all corridors this

close to Christmas, the tracks were never more dangerous, even to experienced track crews. If the mayor decides to send an army of cops below, they would have to be led by qualified track teams. This will take time to coordinate and buy you the extra time you need. To respond to lower levels requires much more diligence and safety concerns. This will cause further delays for an all-out tactical police attack."

"Can you really cause this delay if the mayor orders an immediate incursion?" Micko asked.

"Of course I can. This is federal and private property, and I am in charge of all safety concerns. I am responsible if police officers get electrocuted, run down by trains, attacked by Mole People, or get lost or hurt in dangerous passages. I must have the police led by qualified squads, and this will take time. The mayor can assure the people of New York that everything is being done to resolve this situation, when in reality no one goes below without my authority. I'll call him and advise him of this. You have a few days, Micko, so make them count."

Tiny was furious. His latest victim had escaped and now his hideout was no longer a secret. He placed his suitcase and tool bag into the cart and pushed his way throughout the netherworld, searching for the first sandhog lean-to. Along the way he ran into two Skells.

"Hey mister. That's a pretty nice pushcart you got there," said one bum.

"Can we help you along?" asked the other with a wicked laugh.

Tiny knew what was about to happen, so he struck first. He swung the halogen tool at the first nomad and caught him just above the left ear. The man fell like a dropped brick. He quickly struck the second bum on top of the head with a sickening thud. Blood splattered everywhere as the vagrant's head split like a watermelon.

He stood over his vanquished enemies like a conquering hero, overcome by an incredible adrenaline rush. This was what he was meant to do. Kill adversaries. A better rush than strangling timid women and talking to their decaying bodies.

Tiny wanted all Mole People to know there was a new subterranean conqueror in town, so he sat the corpses back to back in the center of the tracks for all to see.

He was flying high with a new goal: to overcome his fear of the unknown. He would kill Skells and Mole People before they could do him any harm.

Tiny pushed his cart along the narrow concrete floor running parallel to the tracks and tunnel walls, but at a switching junction, the narrow walkway disappeared. The wheeled cart could not be pushed or dragged on the railroad ties or rails, so it was left behind. He had to carry the suitcase and heavy tool bag as he lumbered toward an uninhabited subway station.

Following his father's map, Tiny had to squeeze though a derelict air shaft to reach a set of corroded ladder rungs leading down two stories to another set of train tracks. Tiny had to leave the suitcase behind and go back for it, making a second trip.

Tiny entered the abandoned 34th Street IRT Third Avenue Line subway station. He was exhausted. He remembered what his father had said about this abandoned site. "This train station was deserted in 1955. These rails ran service from the 34th Street Ferry to Grand Central Station and shuttled to Second Avenue."

Although the old-fashioned station was mostly demolished, the sandhog quarters were still habitable. Tiny rested as he drank some water and moved his belongings into the tight rooms. After a quick search, Tiny located an electric source, water, and a small bathhouse.

This place would do for now. Tiny would locate more of these huts and move into the one that best suited his needs. Now he was tired. The adrenaline rush and lugging his baggage had drained him.

Sleep came easy to the killer.

The closest community was the Hanoi Hilton, so Rooster took the woman there. The Mighty Quinn listened intently as Krissy told her tale of terror.

"Rooster, do you think you know where this restaurant is located?" he asked.

"I think so. It's in a dark zone near a spur off the East/West Tunnel," Rooster replied.

Quinn quickly gathered his Outfit together. His men were to sneak up on the Phantom's lair and attack. He trusted his men to capture the killer.

Next he walked Krissy to the fortune teller's tent. He wanted Large Marge to interview her before she received medical attention.

"Large Marge, this is Krissy. She has been through a rough time. I want you to talk to her and give me a sit rep afterward," Quinn said, before he walked off.

"What does he want you to give him?" a shaky Krissy asked.

"A situation report. He wants to know if you are a lying crack whore, an innocent victim, or something in the middle," she replied with a broken toothed smile.

Rooster led a team of five of Quinn's best men in the Outfit. They were armed with metal pipes, knives, and rope.

They stealthily walked to where Rooster thought the hideout was located.

The runner was very familiar with the underground and easily perceived when something was amiss. Rooster spotted the cart Tiny had abandoned and the scattered tracks in the soot that covered the walkway. Now they just had to follow the footprints to the Phantom's hideout.

Soon they came upon the displayed bodies of the two derelicts blocking the rails. Rooster recognized them as Skells. Their heads were matted in blood that had barely congealed. A single large rat was gorging on the left ear of one of the corpses. Flies were feeding and maggots would soon appear.

"This is a fresh kill, Jerry," Tom said.

"This guy has lost it. He's getting off on the thrill of the kill," Jerry replied.

Rooster was advised by Tom to get word to Hannity's Raiders to collect the bodies and dispose of them quickly. He promised to do so right after they pounced on the Phantom.

Tiny had left his place in such a rush that he didn't take the time to search for the correct key to lock the front door. He had taken the padlock with him to secure his new residence.

The Outfit did a quick reconnaissance of the restaurant and determined that the only way in was through a small, rear vent or the front door.

The Outfit decided to rush the front of the location and overpower their quarry with overwhelming manpower. They first entered the colossal hallway leading to the dining area. When the Outfit was sure the location was secure, they entered the kitchen area and observed recent activity. Pots and pans were strewn about along with plates and utensils soaking in the sink.

The vigilantes entered the servants' living quarters and easily determined someone had been living there recently. As they expanded their search, it became evident the Phantom had left in a hurry.

"Tom, down here," Jerry whispered.

The gang joined Jerry at the door to the large, walk-in freezer. With their baton weapons held high, the Outfit entered the gigantic refrigerator. First thing they saw was the bed to their left.

"Why would anyone sleep in a freezer?" Jerry asked.

Tom silently shook his head as they moved forward.

After walking down three steps, they observed a table with three figures sitting to their right. "Don't move, we have you covered!" Tom said.

It took several seconds before the members of the Outfit realized the figures were not a danger. Rooster walked behind the soldiers, not understanding why they had lowered their weapons. Pushing past the larger men, he took a closer look at the three forms sitting at the table. Frost covered the holiday clothing of three ladies who would not be celebrating this Christmas.

"There's another one back here," Tom said.

The group walked to the rear of the freezer and found the old lady hanging from the overhead hooks. Her head was pitched forward, looking down on the group. One glassy eyeball sat in its socket while the other protruded, held only by a frosty tendon. The grossly swollen, purple tongue was fully extended and covered with a light film of ice.

Rooster vomited violently. One of the soldiers helped him to the extra chair at the ladies' table. Rooster sat with his head down in his hands until he regained his composure. When he looked up and viewed the three frozen ladies close up as they sat directly in front of him, heads dangling awkwardly, Rooster retched again.

The Outfit located the small vent that Krissy had escaped through, confirming part of her story. Tom and Jerry led the Outfit back to the Hanoi Hilton as Rooster took off to Hannity's Manor to report the two bodies that needed removal to the Waste Way.

Micko rested well, called Esmeralda, and had a lively conversation with her about the different directions of the case. They both agreed he should drop the Nutty Irishman subterfuge and come clean about being a cop. He could assure the secret societies he would not reveal their existence as long as they continued to covertly work with Blackjack Randazzo and the other Amtrak Police.

He was bothered by something Captain Pedone had mentioned. Pedone warned Micko not to go down to the bedrock level at the west side because work crews were about to begin construction on the Gateway Project. This would include blasting through bedrock under the Hudson River west into New Jersey. Several train lines had been diverted to avoid inference from the blasting crews.

The only two secret societies Micko did not visit were the Morlock Nation and Papa Miller's Lost Souls. Time was running out, so he decided to visit the Morlocks before the excavation began since they lived in the lowest bedrock section. He could always go east to visit Papa Miller later. Besides, Jimmy Joe never heard of Tiny so he probably didn't frequent the east side where the Lost Souls resided.

Micko carefully perused his maps and realized the only way

to get to the Morlock Nation was to take the hidden elevator behind the loading dock area. This ancient elevator went as far down as one could ride.

He carefully stocked his knapsack with necessary items for the trip and surreptitiously snaked his way through Penn Station to reach the loading dock and the elevator.

The lift was dated but did have regular use to some of the upper levels. This was for crews to gain access to work areas. Tracks were routinely maintained, light bulbs replaced, and general maintenance overseen throughout the underground train system.

Micko pressed the lowest sub-basement button and nervously held onto the handrail as the elevator shook and bucked its way to the lowest level. Rooster told him about this ride and the winch leading down a silo to the bedrock.

The edgy cop stepped out of the elevator into a sea of inky darkness. He pulled out his powerful flashlight and easily spotted the medieval-looking winch.

I can't go down that prehistoric thing. It would never hold my weight.

Shining the flashlight down the shaft revealed a large set of rusty ladder rungs leading down the crumbling walls.

Hell, I've come this far, so I might as well climb down.

Micko slid over the edge of the pit and away from the winch. He placed the flashlight in his mouth as he lowered himself onto the first metal rung. As he continued, he would step down one rung, take the light out of his mouth, and shine it to see the next lower rung. After several of these tedious interactions, he decided to go down the ladder keeping the flashlight in his mouth.

This decision nearly cost him his life as the very next ladder rung rested on the crater wall vertically instead of horizontally.

Micko's foot felt the step but instantly knew something was wrong. The mortar that attached the rung to the wall had corroded so much that one side of the ladder was intact while the other side hung loose.

He lost his footing and hung by his hands as his feet swung awkwardly, anxiously looking for a foothold. He dangerously hung on with one hand as he grabbed the flashlight from his mouth with the other. He shined it below and saw that the next intact ladder step was four feet below the broken one. Each rung was set four feet apart.

Starting to lose his grip, Micko made the decision to drop past the broken step and hope to land on the lower one while scraping his hands and feet along the silo wall to slow his fall.

He placed the flashlight back into his mouth and let go. He slid down the wall with his shoes kicking up a cloud of loose concrete. Micko's left foot made contact with the lower step as his hands grasped the broken rung above. In a moment, his right foot also landed on the rusty ladder rung.

Micko paused for a minute to catch his breath and regain his composure. This time he went back to the wearisome process of looking down for the next ladder step, then replacing the flashlight in his mouth and lowering himself. Fortunately, the rest of the ladder rungs were intact and held his weight.

Eventually Micko landed on the soft, sandy bottom of the pit. There was no light at this level. He shined his beam to and fro and noticed horseshoe-shaped bedrock walls blasted eons ago.

He had no idea which way to go, so he walked slowly in a westerly direction, keeping the rugged wall to his right. As he walked, it felt and sounded like walking on broken glass. Micko bent down to examine the sandy floor and realized he was stepping on old, crushed oyster shells.

The detective remembered reading about early NYC being built on oyster beds as a foundation. Rooster traded for oysters with the Morlocks, so this all made sense. He was at the lowest level in Manhattan.

Micko was very quiet. Since he didn't use the noisy winch, he hoped the Morlocks were not aware of his presence. He shined his light above and knew the ceiling was about seven feet high and the opposite wall was a mere three feet away. He had no idea what this primeval hallway was used for.

He walked along the oyster bed until the tunnel took a steep left turn. Instantly, he glimpsed light at the end of the tunnel. He thought this should empty close to the Hudson River.

Suddenly, he froze as a loud engine raced by and the entire hallway shook violently. Loose sand and dust fell from above. In seconds, all returned to normal and he realized a commuter train had just passed overhead.

Micko exited the corridor and it ran directly under the Hudson Line railroad tracks and emptied into the Hudson River as he had expected. What he didn't expect was to see strange-looking dwarfs at the river's edge.

They were off to his right about a hundred yards away, so he couldn't see them clearly. They hauled in a fishing net and removed objects from it. He didn't know if it was crabs, oysters, or fish, but the tiny group worked well together.

He watched as they grabbed several gunny sacks and disappeared around a rocky knoll. It was a cloudy, moonless night, so visibility was poor. Micko decided to climb down the shallow rocky hillside to take a better look.

Poor judgment was the rule of the night. He left his flashlight off so he wouldn't give his presence away. This was smart, but tumbling twenty feet down the dark, slippery moss covered bluff was not.

Micko brushed himself off and retrieved his backpack while shaking his head. *People this stupid should not be allowed to live.*

Realizing the fishermen would have to be deaf not to have heard him, he decided to use his light as he worked his way around the slippery rocks to their last location.

Gone! The small people had entered a small, narrow drainage pipe that stood four feet high and three feet wide. A steady flow of water ran out of this channel, so Micko knew his feet would get wet when he entered.

Entering the sewer pipe was easy, but controlling his balance was a task. Luckily the drain was one of the older ribbed pipes allowing a grip for the hands. The cylinder angled upward at about a three degree angle and the water constantly flowed.

Micko again kept the flashlight in his mouth while his hands gripped along the ribbed walls and his wide-foot stance kept his balance. Soon the angle of the pipeline increased upward, making it more difficult to climb in a hunched over position.

Soon he viewed another aqueduct joining from the left side. This channel appeared to be level, so Micko entered. It was easier to walk through, and Micko hoped the little people took this route.

Now that his path was smoother, he wrinkled his nose at the strong stench inside the tube. At first he thought it might be dead fish, then realized it was a combination of dead fish and animals.

Did these creatures hunt dogs, cats, and fish for sustenance? Did they flush away the remains through this ancient aqueduct system?

As he walked through the putrid-smelling pipe, he observed many other smaller conduits joining in from either side. This watery maze of aqueducts was all connected like a giant spider web.

Eventually he came to an open dungeon with a pool of water overflowing into the drainage pipes. *This must be where the Hudson River's high tide flows and empties during the change of tides.*

Unexpectedly, his flashlight caught gleams of white reflecting off the floor at the reservoir's edge. Human bones . . . as far as the light beam shone! Being a detective, he had seen many skeletons, but even a novice would recognize the human skulls and pelvis bones surrounded by femur bones. The sandy floor was littered with dismembered hands and feet.

"What the hell!" he gasped.

Something made the detective look upward and it all became crystal clear. He was standing at the bottom of Waste Way!

High above was an air shaft that was probably the one Hannity used to dispose of all waste, including the underground dead. The incredibly vile stench was a combination of rancid river water, human waste, dead bodies, and fish products.

He spotted smaller bones that could have been cats, dogs and rats. This was a mass grave site. Micko knew, no matter what happened with the Phantom, this site must be dug up and the remains identified.

Micko shined his light across the vast aqueduct to another hallway on the far left side of the room. He cautiously entered the massive cave on the other end of the darkened hall.

He pulled out his map. He had entered another No Go Zone. In the border of the red-lined area of the map he saw the words, Smugglers' Cove.

The walls and floor were covered in light dust. Cobwebs covered deserted, blocked doorways. The remains of a couple of decaying wooden strongboxes sat in one corner and a large wooden barrel in another.

Micko spotted a long cement ramp and followed it to where it dropped off above the west side train tracks. It was obvious how important this Smugglers' Cove was to burglars in the past.

He made some notations on his map and returned it to the pocket in his backpack. Micko wanted to have another look at the discarded bones in the rancid aqueduct, so he went back into the wet graveyard.

Suddenly, the entire cave shook violently as a loud explosion came from the northern side of the labyrinth. The aqueduct pool vibrated violently and deposited a huge amount of water over its edge that hit Micko like a wave. He and the flood of water cascaded down through the aqueduct maze of pipelines and flew out of the drainage duct and into the Hudson River.

CHAPTER

14

Tiny was in a state of euphoria. He followed his maps and located several sandhog living quarters and spread his clothing out between them. He no longer missed his red-scarfed ladies. He followed his strong urges to kill. He felt energized and renewed after each kill.

His latest victim was a strung-out white junkie girl. While following train tracks through uninhabited tunnels, the wretched junkie jumped out from the track line shadows and begged, "Got some?"

Tiny looked at the wench with her bloodshot eyes and sallow face. She stuck out her hand, hoping to receive the drugs she craved. Instead she was rocked by a blow to the side of her head from the murderous halogen tool.

He left her limp body as it sprawled across the tracks for everyone to see. A great feeling of satisfaction and superiority overwhelmed him. This was what he was meant to be, physically superior to underground dwellers.

The third hut he encountered was the largest, well-hidden with electricity inside. He also located a small, working shower room. Tiny decided to live in this location and use the others if he was in flight.

Two hours after cleaning up his new home, Tiny needed to go topside to buy the necessary household items he had left behind—food, water, cleaning supplies, as well as the normal hygiene products one would find in a bathroom.

Tiny emptied his suitcase, carried it to street level on the west side and began his shopping spree. He placed his purchases into the case as he went from store to store to buy necessary items.

Soon the big man was hungry. He could buy anything he wanted, pizza, heroes, or hot sandwiches, or he could go to the Amtrak dining coaches and take what he wanted.

Tiny wanted a frankfurter from Hawkeye's kiosk. Ever since he was denied a hot dog the night Rooster had spotted him, he had an uncontrollable urge for the tasty meal.

His last shopping stop was at a Rite Aid store a few blocks from Hawkeye's stand. He bought soap and shaving equipment and placed it into his now bulging suitcase.

After a short walk to the hot dog stand, he was ready to order and eat.

"Hey, Hawkeye, how about two dogs and a lamb gyro?"

"Coming right up, Tiny. So what have you been up to lately?" Hawkeye asked indifferently.

The big man didn't answer right away. He cautiously studied Hawkeye to see if he was just being friendly or was snooping. Looking up the street, he spotted Rooster entering a dark alley. After paying for the food he merely answered, "Thanks, Hawkeye, I have to catch a train."

He knew Rooster had knowledge of all activities going on both underground and above. Tiny was desperate to find out if the police or Mole People were looking for him.

He quickly walked to the alley Rooster had entered and knew the runner was going down the grating behind the liquor store heading to the lower levels of the BMT subway line.

Rooster stood over the grating, enjoying a marijuana blunt before descending. The alley was a dead end and Rooster nearly shit his pants when Tiny approached.

"Hey, Tiny it's good to see you man. What's up?" he asked.

The big man stared at Rooster while he put the suitcase on the ground and the food into his coat pocket. The unfortunate runner knew he was in big trouble as Tiny grabbed him by the neck.

Tiny choked Rooster until he fell limp to the ground, coughing and gasping for air. "Tell me everything *now!*"

Rooster knew he was minutes from death, so he told Tiny all about the newspapers calling him the Phantom of Penn Station and how the underground mayors were having a meeting early tomorrow morning to plan a hunt for him.

Tiny grinned with satisfaction as he strangled Rooster and positioned the corpse resting on the metal grating. He looked around the huge trash containers and found a dead rat. He placed the rat in Rooster's drooping mouth.

Captain Pedone was surprised at how calm he spoke to the task force coordinators. The mayor of NYC sent one of his aides, Tom Monahan. Chief of Detectives, Dennis Clifford was present along with a deputy director from the FBI, Ed Dolan, and Amtrak CEO John "Happy" Halpin.

Each task force member demanded the others to assign a large contingent of personnel to patrol Penn Station during the Christmas holiday. Pedone already shot down the idea of flooding the subterranean levels with police, for safety reasons. All agreed this was a valid excuse.

Pedone held the meeting in his office in Penn Station and was in control.

"Gentlemen. We definitely cannot launch a hunting expedition in the lower tunnels for the Phantom. This is too dangerous for your officers. I have limited manpower, even with all holidays cancelled for my officers. I am not too popular with my cops right now, but this is the best I can do. Can anyone else deploy officers to cover the train platforms and concourses?"

The nondescript FBI guy answered, "We have absolutely no one available." He didn't give an explanation or excuse, he just blew everyone off.

The mayor's aide quipped, "Chief, can't you have any of New York's Finest available?" His tone was condescending and arrogant.

"The mayor is well aware that this is perhaps the busiest time of the year for the NYPD, and we have multiple targets to protect requiring all available personnel," Chief Clifford responded in an icy tone as he gave the aide an even icier stare.

The four debated this manpower dilemma for three hours until Chief Clifford pondered out loud, "Maybe I can get ahold of the Christmas parade roster of officers on parade duty and order those same officers to be assigned to Penn Station from now until the parade."

All were in agreement to this idea. Officers assigned to parade duty came from all areas of the NYPD. A few came from specific units not considered high priority and others from detective squads across the city. Each squad would lose one detective to be reassigned for the day. Since these officers were considered nonessential for the parade, the chief would make them non-essential for the holiday and be assigned to cover Penn Station.

The NYPD and the Amtrak officers would both patrol Penn Station and help guard the many commuter train platforms. The idea was to prevent the Phantom from grabbing women and taking them below. When the holidays were over, Pedone would draw up an organized search-and-rescue party in the netherworld. Senior track level teams would lead the cops below and flush out the Phantom and locate the kidnapped victims.

This was a plan that all agreed upon. Captain Pedone knew it was an unrealistic one and hoped Micko could end this drama quickly. Both Pedone and Clifford waited for an update from Micko.

Micko floundered in the cold, murky Hudson River for several seconds before he regained his balance and composure. Freezing, he quickly swam back to retrace his steps to the original horseshoe corridor which led him below the freight tracks.

He knew he didn't have much time before hypothermia would set in, so he immediately headed for The Hanoi Hilton. It wasn't a long walk, but his frigid legs felt very heavy. Soon he was in the huge community dome and heard the banging of water pipes indicating a stranger was approaching. Tom and Jerry came out of the shadows and gawked at the wet, Nutty Irishman.

"Don't you know you're supposed to take your clothes off before you go for a swim?" Jerry said.

Tom laughed and said, "You look like a drowned rat."

Micko shot them an evil glare. Tom removed Micko's coat as Jerry wrapped his own around the freezing man. The pair led Micko into the Hanoi Hilton and through a hidden low ceiling archway into an anteroom.

The room was densely furnished with numerous levels of crates, containers, and boxes. Each one had a cat or dog sleeping in them. Some were injured, while others looked like they lived there.

Suddenly, from behind a wall-dividing tapestry, Kitty and Joe appeared. Even in his wet and freezing condition, Micko understood.

"I'll go to Hannity's Manor and get Cotton Top," Tom said.

"I'll get some dry clothing," Jerry stated.

"Run the shower, Joseph, I'll get him undressed," Kitty said.

Once Micko was stripped to his birthday suit, Kitty led him past her bedroom to another hallway and into an unusually clean shower stall. The room was already filling with steam from the hot water. Micko stepped in and was immediately relieved as his body thawed.

Fifteen minutes later, he stepped out of the shower and Joe handed him a towel to dry off. Tom came into the room with an arm full of clothing.

When Micko finished drying, he put on a pair of warm sweatpants, a worn NY Yankees sweatshirt, and a pair of Conrail work overalls.

"Don't zipper those work clothes just yet. I want to redress that wound," Cotton Top ordered, as she entered the room.

She carried a medical box that looked like a fishing tackle case.

Micko silently did as he was told and still shivering, removed his upper clothing to reveal his stab wound.

Cotton Top professionally restored the medical dressing after closely assessing the cut.

"It looks like my original dressing worked well, until you decided to go swimming," she teased.

"I agree, you did a great job bandaging my arm," he said, through shivering lips.

Mouths were agape as his Nutty Irishman accent was replaced with a Bronx accent.

"I'm a cop searching for the Phantom. I'm sorry for the subterfuge, but I thought it was necessary," he said.

It took several minutes for this to sink in to the small crowd in Kitty's bedroom.

Tom and Jerry had a private conversation, then turned toward Micko and Tom said, "It makes perfect sense to us."

Kitty just smiled, so Micko thought that Joe had probably shared the secret with her earlier as lovers are apt to do.

"Come and sit here, and we'll cover you with extra blankets. You're still shivering," Kitty said.

She led him back to the cat room and sat him in a low beach chair. She piled warm blankets around him. The chill finally left his body as the detective fell into a deep sleep.

Tiny was enraged. He always knew the aboveground police were looking for him, but now he knew the belowground communities wanted to capture him as well.

He thought for a long time about how he should handle this situation. Finally, he made a decision to help him conquer his enemies. Rooster had told him the mayors would meet on the abandoned railway tracks near Shantytown. He knew about the many corridors, hallways, and tunnels that converged there.

Tiny was also familiar with the once-active tracks running into the long vacant area. He studied his father's maps and knew what he needed to do. He walked down to a lower level at the 34th Street and Eighth Avenue subway line adjacent to Penn Station.

His father had brought him here often, since this was now used as a storage and repair station for work trains. Most platforms and facilities were abandoned, except for the repair garage and work trains located off on a side spur of track. From this area, the work trains entered any line of tracks between Penn Station and Grand Central Station.

Mr. Collins had often let Tiny and his father ride in the cab of his work train, so Tiny was familiar with it and its operation. The three rode all over the vast underground rail system, both for work and fun.

Tiny searched through the still-active repair garage until he found the barrels he needed. He slow-rolled the six 55-gallon benzene drums onto the front balcony of the work train. He used industrial strength bungee cords to secure them in place.

Next he carried six propane tanks and also fastened them to the front deck of the locomotive. Tiny was high as a kite on an adrenaline rush. He knew what needed to be done and was getting a thrill out of it.

When he had his rolling bomb in place, he quickly walked along the rail tracks and threw the proper switches that would direct him to the intersection heading toward Shantytown. The ancient track switches had to be manually thrown and directed. The newer ones could be switched electronically from the main control tower.

Tiny secretively crept up on the main track switching station. He had never physically been here before, so he didn't know if the switch was thrown toward the Hanoi Hilton on the left or toward Shantytown on the right.

When he sneaked up to the switching station, he knew it led to Shantytown. He was pleased and walked back the way he had come, rechecking that the switches were in their proper directions.

He would have a deadly surprise for the many mayors tomorrow during their meeting to capture him. Tiny never felt more alive.

Suddenly a huge explosion rocked the entire tunnel system. Debris shot out of thousands of fissures from floor to high ceiling. He knew it was the Gateway Project. The work must have been approved.

His father had told him there were plans to build another train tunnel under the Hudson River to New Jersey. The Gateway Project was the expansion and renovation of the Northeast Corridor rail line between Newark and New York City. The proposed project would cost about $20 billion and would be completed in 2026.

Tiny's father never thought money would be allocated for such an adventurous program, so it was a dead issue. This explosion was either a tragic accident or the beginning of the project's expansion program.

He had to investigate immediately, so he headed north along a north/south tunnel system toward the runaways' rotunda.

Tiny knew where the engineers and tunnel workers stored their construction vehicles.

In fifteen minutes, he was hiding in the shadows, watching a beehive of activity in the once-dormant tunnel. Enormous construction front-loaders and cranes removed tons of bedrock demolished from the blast. A humongous boring machine sat off to the side of the exploded tunnel.

He observed two workers standing near a hut marked *Danger! Explosives!* in large red letters. Tiny knew what had to be done and quickly returned to his new sandhog home.

Micko slept until a deafening explosion woke him up. "What the hell was that?" he called out to no one in particular.

"It's the Gateway Project. The work crews are blasting through the bedrock. They intend to go under the Hudson River to the Jersey side and connect a new rail system," Joe answered.

Now awake, Micko explained how he got dumped into the freezing Hudson. The blasting caused sitting water to shake and flow like a mini tsunami. Many of the water-filled aqueducts would begin to flood and endanger the underground communities.

"Joe, where are my maps?" he asked.

"Don't worry, they are drying out nicely. Too bad your clothes are not," he said.

Micko was comfortable. His body temperature had returned to normal, so he removed the many blankets covering him.

"The entire veteran community pitched in to keep you warm. I don't know what you did to become popular with them, but they all helped," Joe said.

"They are a great bunch of guys, even if they are non-conformist," Micko said. "I have to get to Captain Pedone and stop the blasting. You guys might all get flooded and the Morlock Nation is down at the bedrock level. We have to avoid a dangerous confrontation."

Micko tried to stand up, but half a dozen cats sat on his lap, shoulders, and feet. They had enjoyed the warmth of the blankets and his body heat.

Joe smiled as the cop gently picked up each cat and gingerly placed it in an empty box. He also knew about the dynamite blasting dangers. The Hanoi Hilton's dome showed a huge crack, and tons of debris fell upon the community after each blast. He never thought about the possibility of mass flooding if walls and tunnels were breached.

Micko thanked Joe for all his help and walked through the community to search out his benefactors. The Mighty Quinn was the first to welcome him back to the commune. "The Hudson River gets mighty cold this time of year."

Micko just smiled and gave his pal a man hug. Then he spotted Kitty and he greeted her with a warm hug. "Thanks, Kitty."

"It was our pleasure, detective," she answered.

Quinn walked with him as he entered the MASH tent. Cotton Top had not returned to Hannity Manor yet. She had decided to do checkups on the MASH patients. Micko thanked her.

"Watch that arm for infection," she warned with a smile.

"Detective, I want you to meet Krissy. She has quite a tale to tell," Quinn said.

Micko gave the scraggly woman a quick look over and knew she was a strung-out junkie. "Hi, my name is Detective Mick O'Shaughnessy, Micko for short," he said as he held out his hand to the waif.

"I'm Krissy and some big guy kidnapped me from under Platform 9."

She explained to the detective all that occurred and then fell into a crying fit. Although the woman was filthy and her face covered in dried blood, Micko held her close to comfort her as she sobbed in his arms.

"Micko? Your name is Micko?" Quinn asked.

"Hey, it's better than the Mighty Quinn."

With this comical banter, Krissy let out a gentle laugh and pulled back from Micko.

Quinn related to Micko all that Tom and Jerry reported from Krissy's prison, and how the dead bodies were piling up.

The harried detective ran his fingers through his hair in dismay as he listened. The homicidal Phantom must be caught quickly and the blasting had to be stopped.

"The mayors are all meeting at 7 a.m. tomorrow morning where the maze of catacombs meets near Shantytown. This will help facilitate the apprehension of the Phantom," Quinn said.

"Great, then I'll concentrate on postponing the blasting on the west side, until we can safely relocate the endangered communities," Micko said.

At Quinn's orders, Tom and Jerry escorted a wobbly Micko back to Penn Station. From there he hurried to his hidden hotel room.

Luckily, Chief Pedone had stocked some sandwiches and beer in the mini fridge. Micko ate while retrieving his phone, gun, and badge from the small safe. He was going to be armed from this point on. The Nutty Irishman subterfuge was over. He was Detective O'Shaughnessy from now until the Phantom was stopped.

CHAPTER
15

Tiny raced back to his new sandhog home and retrieved his suitcase. He had already emptied out the hygiene and household items just purchased. With the bag and halogen tool, he trekked back to the construction site.

He hid in the shadows of a big dirt mound removed from the newly blasted tunnel. There was a lot of activity as portable lights kept the construction site well-lit for twenty-four-hour excavation.

Like his earlier visit, two workmen guarded the *Danger! Explosives!* hut stationed in the shadows. Tiny watched the men and the construction activity until one of the guards walked away from the shed and hid behind a bright yellow dump truck. Tiny could see the glow of a cigarette and decided to make his move.

The remaining workman was busy texting on his cell phone as Tiny casually walked toward him. The big man feigned walking past the unobservant guard and swiftly struck a deadly blow with the halogen tool.

Tiny dragged the dead guard to the rear of the explosives shack and concealed the body under a large blue tarp. Rapidly, he used the halogen bar to remove the lock and hinge. In seconds, the clasp tore off and the door opened.

As soon as the suitcase was filled with stacks of dynamite, fuse wire, and blasting caps, the thief sneaked out into the darkness and back to the work train repair garage. The smoking guard was oblivious to these actions.

Tiny sat in the maintenance room and attached the fuses and blasting caps to the bundles of dynamite sticks. The work crew kept the sticks in plastic bags and wrapped them in cardboard for safe storage.

He had watched work crews blow a section of train tracks a few years ago. His father and Mr. Collins had explained the details of the operation since Tiny asked many questions.

He had five bundles of six sticks. Each bundle was taped together with fuses connecting each to a blasting cap. The fuses were then connected to one main wick. Tiny was taught that this was the easiest way to use dynamite.

Mr. Collins had explained the complicated way, which included drilling holes into rock and using battery-operated fuses for safety reasons, but Tiny couldn't follow the concept or logic. He did understand how to attach a blasting cap and fuse into a stick of dynamite and light the fuse. Nothing could be simpler.

Now, Tiny duct-taped the five explosive bundles to the benzene drums and propane tanks on the front of the maintenance locomotive. He had just one wick to light and all fuses would ignite the blasting caps simultaneously.

He climbed into the locomotives cab, looked it over, and remembered everything Mr. Collins had taught him about running an engine. He made sure the brake lever was in the first notch, indicating it was in full brake position. Next, he made sure the throttle was also in the first notch position, and the gear lever was set in neutral.

Tiny checked under the seat cushion and the starter key was where Mr. Collins always kept it. He removed the key, placed it into the instrument start position, and pressed the locomotives start button. Everything was in good working order for his deadly plan in the morning.

Micko called Chief Clifford and informed him of the latest events. Clifford was very interested about the Waste Way bone collection site. He also advised his detective how Pedone's attempt to delay the hunt for the Phantom underground had failed. The mayor had caved to public pressure for an immediate arrest. With or without safety crews, a large task force would scour the labyrinths beneath Penn Station for the killer. Also, his plans for extra police protection at Penn Station's train platforms fell apart. Only the task force would be added.

Knowing that protesting would be useless, Micko warned his boss about the dangers of the blasting near the Hudson River train yards. Disrupting the underground communities could cause havoc if they ran topside to avoid flooding and ceiling and wall collapses. This environmental hazard could also endanger the task force officers.

"I will talk to the mayor about this, but he is determined to capture the Phantom immediately and probably won't listen to me," Clifford said.

"Do your best, Chief, and I'll also call Captain Pedone and ask him to do all he can to stop the explosions until we can reevaluate the underground situation and capture the killer," Micko said.

The two spoke for another hour about the recent events in the catacombs. Micko was exhausted and needed sleep badly, but he still had to call Pedone and end the night with a call to Esmeralda.

His conversation with Pedone was fruitless. The captain had no power to stop the excavation work on the new tunnel. "Hell, Micko, I don't even have the power to prevent the task force from racing into extreme danger below," Pedone said.

Micko called Esmeralda and had a light-hearted conversation before she asked him what was really going on. He updated her on the nefarious situation and she said, "This is your assignment, and only you can handle it without disaster."

The weary detective knew she was right and drifted off to sleep with a half-full can of beer on his nightstand along with the remains of a half-eaten sandwich.

At 6:00 a.m., the Mighty Quinn and Hannity shook hands at the mayors' meeting place. They were the closest to the summit site and arrived early.

"Did you hear about Rooster?" Hannity asked.

"No, we had some excitement at the Hanoi Hilton yesterday,

but not a word about Rooster. What happened?"

"One of the other runners, Radio, found him dead in an alley posed on top of one of our entrance gratings with a dead rat stuck in his mouth," Hannity replied.

"Well, I guess the Phantom is sending us a message, loud and clear," Quinn said.

One by one, the other mayors arrived and all were in an unusually friendly mood. The seriousness of the situation allowed them to put personal differences aside. The depraved demise of Rooster was a shock. The Phantom and the constant Gateway Project blasting endangered every underground community. Even Jimmy Joe from the Waldorf Astoria Gays and Papa Miller from the east side Lost Souls arrived. A few members of the Section 8s stood on the periphery along with a few of the Rotunda Kids.

The Shantytown residents had nothing to do with members of organized communities. They were the outcasts of outcasts. The only reason they allowed these rare mayor meetings near their shanty village was because they were vastly outnumbered.

The Skells and the Morlocks were not invited, but the disastrous blasting affected their communities the most. The Skells lived just above the bedrock where the detonating had a devastating effect. Since they lived scattered about and without decent hovels, the shock waves caused water leaks and excessive dust to infiltrate their filthy tunnels.

The Morlocks lived in quiet secrecy close to the construction site. No one knew they were in the vicinity of the explosions. Since they lived in almost total darkness, the Morlocks developed a keen sense of hearing. The noise from the barrage of dynamiting was deafening to them.

They tried to escape a collapsed tunnel and ran into the blinding portable lights of the construction crews. Hopelessly confused, the Morlock Nation gathered to seek an escape from this impossible situation.

Although they had lived in the bedrock region underground for generations, occasionally an adventurous troglodyte would explore and find airways and shafts steering to above levels. This would lead to dangerous tunnels, sewers, and ancient passages. Now at a hasty gathering, these daring Morlocks would lead the others to higher ground in an effort to avoid the construction devastation.

Micko was the last to arrive. The stabbing, long explorations, and being dumped into the frigid Hudson River had taken its toll. He overslept. He offered his apologies and Hannity declared the meeting in order.

Tiny's excitement level had peaked. He was awake and ready to roll. He had a plan and now he wanted to execute it. He double-checked his explosives and their connections to the locomotive's front bumper. He cautiously opened the primary seal on the drums of benzene.

He removed a large bungee cord, tied one end around the train's throttle lever, and placed a cigarette lighter on the driver's console. One last look around and he was ready.

The ignition key was removed from under the engineer's seat and turned to the ON position. Tiny double-checked the position of the three levers before pressing the engine start button. The old work locomotive purred like a kitten.

Tiny slowly released the brake and put the gear lever into forward. He was standing while he performed these functions. Now he sat in the engineer's driver's seat to get comfortable. Once he felt relaxed, Tiny pulled the throttle back one notch.

The prehistoric train bucked twice, then slowly moved forward. Tiny's excitement level rose. He pulled the throttle to the second of eight notches. The locomotive crawled along as Tiny guided the beast through several early switch changes.

These shifts were necessary to get Tiny on the set of tracks that he desired. He had to carefully navigate through a set of active freight and subway lines. The track lights were of great importance. He could not travel against a red light or the main subway switchboard would know and take action against him. If he followed the safety rules, the main tower wouldn't detect him until his mission was accomplished.

Luckily, he entered several tunnels without incident. The train wheels squealed loudly when he left the main rail system and entered deserted lines. The tracks were covered in a variety of filth, including brake dust.

The screeching wheels awakened cats, dogs, and track rabbits as well as vagrants sleeping in the off-track hollows. He put the train up one more notch as he entered a straightaway on a stretch of track that hadn't seen a locomotive in many years.

Tiny knew when it was time to slow the iron horse down to one notch as he neared the perpendicular east/west switch just south of the massive tunnel to Hannity's Manor and Shantytown.

It was a ninety-degree turn, so Tiny had the train crawling as it entered the switching station from one train line to another. He masterfully guided the locomotive through the tight turn and immediately turned the throttle up two notches. While the train picked up speed, he climbed out of the cab and walked to the front of the engine and lit the main fuse to the explosives.

When he cautiously arrived back into the cab, he throttled up another notch, grabbed the throttle bungee cord, and stepped out on the cab's outside ladder and guardrail. As the train picked up speed, he pulled the cord, which kicked the throttle up another notch, and he jumped off the train and did a semi-controlled roll along the trackside gutter.

When he stopped tumbling along the trackside walkway, he ran as fast as he could back to the intersection and the switching station.

The construction crew for the Gateway Project were busy assembling a dynamite blast to remove a wall of solid rock. Several engineers argued over the size of the explosives to be used. They finally agreed and the site was cleared of all work crews as the ignition would be set electronically from a safe distance.

Diesel truck horns blasted warnings for a full two minutes prior to detonation. Safety was their number one concern, when it should also have been the size of the explosives.

Captain Pedone was very uncomfortable. He was hosting the mayor, the NYPD chief of detectives, the assistant director of the New York branch of the FBI, as well as high ranking Amtrak officials. They all wanted to be onsite and give a talk to the task force officers about to descend into the treacherous maze below Penn Station.

The news media were on hand to take pictures and record the event so they could sensationalize it later in their studios. Captain Pedone's Amtrak Police Headquarters was turned into a publicity circus, and he was not amused. He still feared for the safety of anyone venturing into uncharted territory far below the surface of Penn Station. The task force didn't have maps or schematics to follow. They would probably wander aimlessly until they all got lost. Pedone would have to organize another task force to help locate the first task force. This was insane.

The mayor was the first to boost the egos of the twenty officers who would attempt to flush out the Phantom. Encouragement was one thing, knowledge was another. This was tantamount to sending officers from the cornfields of Oklahoma into the mean streets of Harlem.

Few of the task force members had ever been more than two levels underground, no less ten levels to the bedrock. Pedone knew this was an accident waiting to happen, but he was overruled by higher ups in the administration.

The meeting of the mayors representing the organized underground communities was harmonious until Micko arrived. Several of the mayors objected to his subterfuge as a homeless person to gain information.

Micko decided to step back and allow Quinn to explain on his behalf. His own explanation would only increase the quarrelling. As he stood in the middle of the two sets of tracks that ran through this tunnel line, he noticed vibrations along the rails.

The arguing had risen to a deafening crescendo, but Micko knew something else was wrong. *Abandoned tracks don't vibrate.* Looking east, he saw Shantytown and the collapsed tunnel wall that dead-ended this corridor.

Looking north, he saw the catacombs leading to Hannity's Manor. The pair of tracks running west went to the Hudson River and the Hudson Train Line.

Suddenly, he knew what was causing the rails to shake. A single locomotive crept past the intersection at the switching station and entered this tunnel from the south. Micko watched as the train engine picked up speed and rushed east toward them. It wasn't until a large figure jumped from the train and ran back to the intersecting junction that he realized the danger.

"Runaway train! Runaway train! Get off the tracks, get off the tracks!" he shouted.

The hostile crowd of mayors and other spectators stopped yelling and looked at the mighty engine bearing down on them and confused looks replaced the anger on their faces. The racing train was almost upon them before they realized its evil intent.

Micko physically grabbed Quinn and pulled him along the track gully toward the out-of-control train. Guessing what was about to happen, he headed toward the same intersecting tunnel that the big man ran to.

As the racing train careened past them, they both saw the explosives strapped to the front of the train's cab. Realizing the inevitable, Quinn pulled free from Micko so they could both run faster.

When the pair reached the corner of the North/South-bound Tunnel, they watched in horror as the train raced past the horror-stricken mayors and smashed through Shantytown. Tents were ripped and trailed the screeching engine like torn parachutes. Boiling pots and furniture were knocked over and clotheslines ripped apart, as most of the hovels were completely destroyed. The residents were unaware of the oncoming train until it was too late. They had no time to evacuate or take any kind of evasive action. The train just barreled through their poverty-stricken village.

Micko watched as the mayors and their followers fled into the numerous catacombs that led into the meeting hall tunnel from every direction. Most made it into the passages, but they couldn't escape the horrors to come.

The runaway train smashed through the village and rammed into the collapsed wall. The wall was not straight up and down but collapsed at an angle. The engine ran up the wall like a steep ramp. It separated from the tracks, rose up the wall, and was eerily suspended for a lingering moment.

Next came the horrible series of explosions. The first explosion sent an immense rush of hot air into Micko and Quinn's faces. They covered up and looked back as another explosion sent barrels of benzene flying through the air.

The ceiling at the dead-end wall began to collapse in a fiery rush on top of the remains of the locomotive. A colossal wall of flame engulfed the entire area. Blazing drums landed in Shanty-town, turning it into an inferno. Most of the makeshift shelters were made of cheap wood, paper, and plastic. Within moments, only a sea of flames remained where the village once stood.

Shantytown residents screamed in pain and horror as they ran covered in burning benzene. Each explosion sent drums of boiling benzene everywhere, even into the maze of catacombs where the mayors sought safety. Soon shrieks of horror and pain emanated from the flaming hallways.

Micko and Quinn watched helplessly as human torches dashed about, lit up like Roman candles. Horrifying cries of agonizing death filled the incinerating cavern. Appalling shrieks of torturous pain echoed throughout the various tributaries of the catacomb maze where the mayors and spectators had fled.

An entire wall of rock blocking the east end of the cave was now completely collapsed, and a series of huge pipes could be seen through the fiery blaze near the now upside down locomotive.

The makeshift Shantytown was utterly destroyed, and all that remained were the burned victims lying in ghastly fetal positions scattered all about the former village.

The painful cries for help were still echoing from the catacomb vestibules when a wall of rats raced out from the felled wall at the east end of the cavern, near the twisted remains of the locomotive. The rodents fled the fires engulfing the huge cave and its arteries. They headed in the direction of Hannity's Manor.

"Micko, I must go and help those people!" Quinn yelled over the noise of the chaotic scene.

"I'm going after the Phantom," Micko said.

The two raced off in different directions. Quinn ran north in the middle of the rat swarm. Micko raced west in the direction of the Phantom.

Everything happened so quickly and as Micko tried to get the ghastly images out of his head, he spotted the big man ahead. The Phantom was limping. He must have hurt himself jumping from the speeding locomotive.

Micko stayed in the shadows of the track gullies as he caught up to his foe. He felt into his coat pocket where he had placed his .380 automatic pistol.

Suddenly the Phantom turned back and stared at where Micko hastily crouched. He looked straight at Micko and a devilish smile crossed his face as he waved his halogen tool in a menacing manner.

Micko knew he was exposed, as he drew his weapon from his coat pocket. The Phantom made a quick move and darted into a doorway, and Micko lost sight of him. This part of the tracks was dimly lit, and Micko held off using his flashlight in an attempt to conceal his presence. Now that the Phantom knew he was being chased, the cop needed to use the light to enter the darkness of this entranceway.

As he neared the spot where he last saw his prey, Micko had a strange feeling he was being followed. *Could the Phantom have an accomplice?*

The detective stood still for a minute thinking of his options. He quickly decided to continue chasing the Phantom and be aware there might be an enemy pursuing him.

With flashlight illuminating the doorway, Micko cautiously entered. He feared being struck by the crowbar the Phantom wielded. The entryway led to a set of spiral stairs and emptied into a large, rusty, drain pipe.

A swift glance showed the big man's wet footprints as he raced further west along this conduit. Water and trash rushed through the middle of this channel and footprints were easy to spot. The cylinder twisted every six to ten feet, so Micko could not see his adversary but knew he was just ahead.

Smaller water-filled tributaries entered this large pipe from both the right and left. Micko had to slow down as he approached each of these intersecting sewers, not knowing if the Phantom waited.

Eventually he came upon a horseshoe-shaped cave on his right that looked familiar. The wary detective slowly approached and observed more wet footprints leading in that direction. Cautiously, he left the large sewer and entered the cave that he recognized as Smugglers' Cove. The footprints headed into a tunnel on the west side of the cove. Entering the lair, he noticed the tunnel was wide at first and narrowed the farther he went. Steam pipes lined the wall to his left. They noisily flushed hot steam from cracks and leaks. This cave was made from stone, and the escaping steam covered the ground with a slippery wet mist.

Micko could not see or hear his prey, and this unnerved him. Many small apertures and rooms speared off from this narrow steam pipe tunnel, and the Phantom could be lurking in any one of them.

He tightened the grip on his pistol and held it at the ready as he proceeded forward in the dark passageway with his flashlight in his left hand. The concrete conduit took a hard left turn and as Micko attempted to see around the hidden corner, he never saw the tall figure emerge from the narrow crevice on his right side.

The Phantom rushed out of the fissure with the metal bar raised over his head. He attempted to swing the tool down on Micko's head, but the walls were too cramped and he only hit the detective a glancing blow.

Micko went down hard. His flashlight went one way and his gun went another way. In the semi-darkness, he watched through a sea of blood as his opponent, grinning victoriously, raised the weapon for the death blow.

It was like a slow motion movie as Micko watched the massive Phantom trying to raise the tool in the confined space of the low-ceilinged tunnel. Finally, he angled the tool lower, where he could deliver repeated half swings.

Micko raised his left hand in a defensive posture as the first blow was dealt. He heard the sickening sound of his wrist being shattered. Now nearly unconscious, he raised his right arm to ward off the next strike. Just as the behemoth moved in for the kill, Micko had a final disturbing thought. *What a weird way to die, all alone in a sewer.*

Suddenly, gunshots rang out. The Phantom's body shivered as bullets struck. Both Micko and the Phantom looked at the shooter with astonished expressions. The Gimp! Joe Lombardi was crouched with Micko's pistol in a combat stance.

Now Micko comprehended who was following him. The realization hit home just as the Phantom fell on top of him. The sheer weight of the Phantom knocked the wind out of Micko and as he lay there gasping for air, he watched as Joe and Popeye rolled the big man off him.

"Where the heck did you two come from?" an incredulous Micko gasped.

"We have been following you ever since you went to the mayors' meeting. We worried that they might not like being fooled by your silly Irish disguise," Joe answered.

"Well, thank God you did. This damn Irish shillelagh didn't do me any good. I didn't have time to pull it from my waistband to ward off the blows," he said.

"How do you feel? Your head wound looks nasty and we heard your arm break," Popeye said.

Micko pulled a handkerchief from his pocket and placed it to his bleeding scalp. "Help me up, boys."

"Be careful with your footing. This sewer runs to the ramp leading straight down to the Amtrak passenger tracks along the Hudson Line," Popeye warned.

Micko looked past the prone body of the Phantom and could now see around the corner to the steep incline where the tracks were clearly visible. The early morning light was noticeable at the bottom of the slope. It was the Smugglers' Cove concrete loading ramp.

Without warning, a violent explosion rocked the tunnel system. The force knocked the three men off their feet. *The Gateway Project is blasting*, Micko thought.

Repeatedly, a series of intense explosions shook the entire area, and a cave-in occurred a hundred feet away, in the direction they had just come. Dust, concrete, and dirt flew in all directions.

Micko slowly grabbed his shillelagh and used it to help get back on his feet. The tunnel was now darker as a thick cloud of dust covered everything in sight. Even the emerging daylight was blocked.

The flashlight spears gave off a supernatural glow as tiny particles were illuminated in the dust cloud. The three didn't want to attempt the tricky slide down the steep ramp to the railroad tracks, and their way back was blocked, so they started to look for an outlet from the cave-in.

Suddenly, something grabbed Micko's leg and began pulling him toward the smugglers' ramp. He slipped on the slick moss-covered floor and was being dragged from behind.

The Phantom! He's not dead. Popeye and Joe dashed past the fallen detective and wrestled with Tiny, but he was too strong. The Phantom picked up his halogen tool and swung it at his attackers like a madman. The tool ricocheted off the narrow walls but also smacked off the bodies of Micko's buddies.

Both Joe and Popeye were motionless on the ground as the Phantom staggered to his feet. Micko was lying on his back in the slimy water as the Phantom approached with the crowbar half raised. The giant was silhouetted by rays from the dusty light behind him gleaming into the sewer below the ramp.

In an instant, Micko again pulled the shillelagh from his belt and using it like a spear, stabbed the big man in the chest with the pointed end of the staff.

The strike wasn't enough to hurt the Phantom, but it did knock him off balance and he fell backward into the slimy water, sliding down the vertical ramp and onto the railroad tracks below.

The Phantom, unsteadily, rose to his feet and looked around for his tool. He saw it lying a few feet away, stuck under a railroad tie on the inside of the northbound train tracks.

He picked up the nefarious weapon and looked up at Micko, still lying at the top of the concrete bank. He waved it menacingly at the prone detective.

Micko was in trouble once again. His comrades were badly injured. He was seriously injured. There was no escape from behind and the madman, ahead, was intent on killing him.

The Phantom raised his arms in victory as he took a step toward the ramp leading him up to his victim.

In a flash, a commuter train raced by at 130 mph. In seconds it was gone. This was a minor distraction, as Micko had other things to worry about. He wiped blinding blood from his eyes and strained to see. *Where is the Phantom?*

It took Micko several minutes to realize . . . The Phantom was *everywhere*! Being hit by a train going that fast, the Phantom's body had exploded like a meat balloon. He was everywhere along the northbound Acela Express Line.

The last speaker was just finishing his speech, backslapping the task force members for their impending, heroic adventure into the caves under Penn Station when the first blast rocked the station.

Water pipes burst in every bathroom and sink in the concourse level stores. Within minutes, the waiting area floors were covered in pools of water as shop owners hastily tried to locate cutoff valves. This sent the hidden homeless from the rear alleys out into the open. Commuters feared it was a terrorist attack and ran mindlessly in all directions, slipping and falling on the wet marble floors.

Chief Pedone quickly sized up the situation and ordered, "Every available officer hit the floor immediately and offer assistance to the injured."

The Phantom task force was instantly transformed into a rescue force. It was Christmas Eve, and a huge volume of passengers were fleeing the station as fast as they could in a rare panic. The task force officers extended reassurances and help to those hurt during the confusion.

In rapid succession, three more devastating explosions rocked the terminal. Light fixtures and bulbs crashed down from above. Penn Station's main concourse area was in complete chaos.

More water cascaded out of broken pipes, drenching the floors. Glass windows shattered and a plethora of objects rained down on holiday shoppers from above.

Travelers ran for their lives in pandemonium. An archway leading to the PATH trains to New Jersey collapsed. The escalators leading to street levels stopped working and buckled under the violent shaking from the explosions below.

Suddenly, the rail users stopped running and stood in the waiting area looking for some guidance. They feared running into certain death and waited for the police to lead them to safety.

Ceilings were disintegrating in several train tunnels and a mass of escaping dust and debris flowed out of the platform areas. The train platforms were warped and crumbling, sending hundreds of harried commuters to the apparent safety of the main lounge in front of the information booth.

The Amtrak Police and task force officers attempted to comfort the anxious crowd and assure them it was not a terrorist attack. Police radios advised the officers that a gas explosion was responsible.

The scene was frenzied with distressed travelers mixed with the homeless standing shoulder to shoulder. Then the grimy residents of the underground communities fled aboveground as their villages collapsed and flooded.

Hundreds of Mole People rushed into the waiting area, violently pushing their way past the shocked commuters. Dozens of shoving matches ensued between the vagrants and the upper-class travelers.

It took some time before the anarchy was contained while the police tried to quiet everyone down. The explosions had ceased, the falling debris was minimized, and the flooding seemed controlled. Shop owners distributed water and napkins so the injured could wash their eyes from the soot and dust.

Just as the peace was returning, a crowd of Morlocks scampered out from a long-neglected alley and pressed their way through the crowd. Their hideous appearance scared the mass of holiday shoppers into another panic.

One mob of frightened people ran to the crumpled escalators, others to the collapsed wall leading away from the terminal, while others ran in terror to the dilapidated train platforms.

The Morlocks scampered through the crowd to the main alley behind Dunkin' Donuts. From there, the younger, intrepid explorers led the Morlock Nation down a hidden shaft to lower levels heading east, far from the excavation of the west side. Although the troglodytes were quickly gone, the mayhem continued.

The incredulous police watched in horror as the unsightly dwarf-like creatures waddled like ungainly penguins wearing colorful green 2007 sunglasses above the rims, props from New Year's Eve 2007 in Times Square.

It took hours to restore tranquility in Penn Station. Additional police from the NYPD and Port Authority arrived, along with numerous ambulances and fire trucks. The damaged exits were barricaded and the injured were cared for. Rescuers guided the frenzied travelers up the marble stairs to the street above.

When there was calm, Captain Pedone returned to his office. His phone had been ringing incessantly. There was some type of unlicensed explosion in a west side tunnel rupturing a natural gas line from New Jersey to Manhattan. When the construction crew detonated a planned explosion, the escaping gas multiplied the effects of their explosion and caused a series of follow-up explosions.

Pedone had numerous calls advising him a person had been struck by the Acela Express northbound train. The train engineer made the police notification as it continued on its way to Boston.

While he was processing this new information, he took a new call from the Gimp. Pedone smiled as he listened to what Joe Lombardi had to say.

CHAPTER

16

Micko woke up dazed in a hospital bed. Tubes were stuck into his right arm, and his left arm was in a cast up to his elbow. He was alone in a large single room. He was aware of voices outside his room. He desperately tried to recollect the events preceding his visit to this infirmary. When his head cleared, he decided to have a little fun.

"Hey, what's a guy have to do to get a cheeseburger and a beer in this place?" he hollered.

Immediately, a mob of people entered his room from the outside lobby. A tough nurse instantly took charge. "Wait there." She pointed to the small vestibule as she quickly checked the patient's vitals.

"You're just fine," she snapped and exited the room.

Esmeralda rushed over and hugged him while planting a big kiss on his lips.

"You don't look so tough now, detective," she said.

"Well, you should see the other guy," he said right back.

"We can't find the other guy, just bits and pieces." Chief Clifford laughed.

"Hmm, I guess he really is a phantom," Micko said. "How are Popeye and Joe the Gimp?"

"They are in the next room, and they are doing just fine," Captain Pedone answered. "Each has a broken rib or two with some bumps and bruises."

Pedone told Micko how the three of them escaped the cave-in by dragging each other through flooded sewers in Smugglers' Cove, until The Gimp found a tunnel he recognized. They had staggered through passageways until they wound up in an alley behind a palm reader's shop. From there, Popeye flagged down a passing ambulance, which took them to New York-Presbyterian Allen Hospital at 5141 Broadway.

"You have a nasty concussion, many head stitches, and a broken wrist," Esmeralda chimed in.

"You certainly pulled my fat out of the fire and a promotion is on the way," Chief Clifford said.

"Thank God you got that bastard before the task force tried to go deep underground. Anyway, you made me look like the best cop on the Amtrak Police Department. I received all of the credit for safeguarding over a thousand commuters on Christmas Eve while the terminal was under siege from explosions and panic. I'll probably get a promotion, too," Pedone said.

Captain Pedone explained how the maintenance train explosion completely leveled the collapsed wall in the Shantytown tunnel. Behind the wall was an engineering station that distributed heat and water throughout the Penn Station subterranean tunnels. Gas lines from New Jersey ran under the Hudson River and docked with New York pipes at this junction. These were breached during the explosion. Steam, water, and gas were propelled through numerous caverns, and when the construction crews dynamited their tunnel, the effects were catastrophic. More utility pipes burst, tunnel roofs collapsed, and excessive flooding wiped out all of the underground communities on the west side.

"What about casualties?" Micko asked.

"Terrible. All of Shantytown is gone. Those that survived are in local burn centers. Most of the mayors are dead, burned beyond recognition. My men found the remains of a meth lab in the rubble. I'm sure this added to the conflagration. The shanty villagers must have been selling crystal meth to the topside addicts. The remaining underground dwellers are without leadership. Quinn and his vets are alive but homeless. Hannity survived, but when the rescuers rendered aid, they found a .25 caliber handgun on his person, so he is being treated in the Bellevue Hospital prisoner ward. He has been arrested for possession of an unregistered gun. We are running the serial number of the gun now," Pedone said.

"Captain, check the ballistics from that gun to the ballistic reports from the .25 caliber shooter case from a few years ago," Micko said.

"You're not suggesting Hannity was the .25 caliber shooter?"

"That's exactly what I'm suggesting," Micko said.

FBI Special Agent Buddy Burger entered the room. "How you doing, Micko?"

"Buddy, what the hell are you doing here?"

"I have an anti-terrorist conference meeting in Boston next week, so I thought I'd spend Christmas in New York prior to going up there. You are all over the news again, so I thought I'd try to help out. I always come to you for help, so now I can return the favor."

"What *can* you do to help me? Take away this nagging headache or fix my broken arm?" Micko asked.

"No, I can't do anything about that, but I did have a nice chat with Father Flynn. He told me of your proposal for turning unused Catholic Church property into homeless shelters. I have many influential contacts, so I made a few phone calls, and *they* made a few phone calls.

"The bottom line is, the Catholic Church cannot receive any more bad press. If they refused your proposal, the negative press would be swift and toxic. Especially after the recent events calling attention to the homeless problem underground during Christmas. Even as I speak, the Red Cross is setting up cots with blankets in several unoccupied schools. Army-style cafeterias are cooking hot food, and the governor and mayor are sending outreach counselors and psychiatrists to deal with the homeless and addicts."

Father Flynn entered the room and said, "How are you, my son?"

"With all this support, I'm doing pretty good, Father."

"Well, with the help of your colorful FBI friend and all the media coverage of your heroics and the plight of the homeless, I was able to easily convince the Archbishop of New York to convert the closed schools into selective homeless shelters. The gymnasiums are currently putting up hundreds right now. Construction will begin shortly as each shelter will house specific groups. There are numerous grants and donations being made hourly. People are very generous at Christmastime," he said, with a warm smile.

It was then that Micko observed the bright red Santa, surrounded by palm trees, on the shirt Agent Burger wore. "I don't want you going anywhere near my homeless pals with that shirt, buddy. They're already mad as hatters and that shirt surely won't help," he said.

"What are you talking about? The archbishop loved it and so did a cardinal visiting from Rome," Burger replied with a laugh.

"I don't know where you get those shirts, but I do appreciate the help," Micko said. He turned his attention to his boss. "Chief, what about identifying all those human bones beneath the Waste Way?"

"There's no rush on that. When the Gateway Project crew blasted, they overpowered what they thought was a solid wall of rock. Too much dynamite plus ruptured gas pipes led to quite a destructive outcome. Part of that outcome was the complete devastation of the Waste Way. A small tidal wave of water washed everything right into the Hudson River through dozens of aqueduct tributaries. In due time, I'll have the Chief of Special Operations Bureau get the NYPD Scuba Team suited up for recovery of the remains," he said.

For the remaining Christmas day, Micko greeted friends and colleagues. The conversations were brief as his visitors returned home to spend the holiday with loved ones. The fact that they checked up on him made Micko quite happy.

Later, Captain Pedone returned flashing an ear-to-ear smile. "Micko, you were right. The .25 caliber shooter case is now officially closed. Hannity is our man. How did you know?"

"Several things, Captain. Joe the Gimp told me Hannity kept a .25 revolver hidden in the confines of Hannity's Manor.

I had Esmeralda do a history search on Hannity, and she found out he was defrocked as a criminal defense lawyer for unethical activities. He lived in Sayville, Long Island, and would make the daily commute to Manhattan through Penn Station.

"When he lost his license to practice law, his wife divorced him and took him to the cleaners. He was virtually homeless. This all occurred around the time of the Penn Station .25 caliber shooting spree. I thought maybe Hannity snapped and took out his rage on any commuter he came in contact with. Eventually, the madness subsided long enough for him to figure out he had better stop and hide. Hide he did, in the catacombs underground.

"From there, he developed Hannity's Manor and when he went mental, he publicly flogged disobedient serfs in his feudal society. To me, this was how it all added up," Micko said.

Pedone was ecstatic. He told Micko, "I am going to get credit for closing a serious cold case and you are getting an assist. The commuters who were directly affected by the explosion and the ensuing chaos were not badly injured and gave great credit to the first responders who handled the frenzied situation. Luckily the press didn't give much coverage to the unusual dwarfs that ran through the station to escape the madness below ground.

"The outside media people thought the harried commuters they interviewed were exaggerating in the middle of a panic situation. The members of the press who actually witnessed the Morlocks were wise enough to deny it. They already had a huge story without losing credibility describing alien-like creatures from below."

Pedone continued telling Micko how the Gateway Project was currently placed on hold until new engineers could re-evaluate the dig. Work crews were eager to get at the over-time cash to help clean up Penn Station and the lower tunnels. Arrangements were being made to establish a search-and-rescue mission to the lowest level of the complicated labyrinth below Manhattan. He would oversee much of these operations with the critical acclaim of his bosses who had once criticized him.

"Micko, you have changed my position here at Amtrak. I wouldn't be surprised if the CEO tried to adopt me," he said.

"I wish you could have seen the looks on people's faces when the Morlocks darted across the main concourse area. They were wearing these ridiculous 2007 New Year's Eve-themed sun-glasses. They looked hideous and waddled erratically and scared the hell out of everyone," he chuckled.

"Rooster must have traded those old sunglasses to the Mor-locks for oysters. They can't stand bright light. That must have been quite a sight," Micko said.

Soon Micko was alone with Esmeralda. His guests had departed, leaving the detective feeling appreciated. Then he thought, *I feel appreciated, while my two rescuers sit in a lonely hospital room.*

Micko rang the buzzer to the nurse's station and the big, angry nurse walked in.

Before she could demand an explanation for being dis-turbed, he asked, "Can I have my two pals moved into this room? The chief of detectives was gracious enough to arrange this huge room for my privacy, and now I would like to share it with my friends."

A slow smile crept over the tough nurse's face as she gave a warm nod to the injured detective.

Within an hour, Popeye and the Gimp were moved into Micko's room along with the nurse's station Christmas party.

The angry nurse was now friendly. The patients were not on any special diets, so she fed them cake and holiday snacks. One nurse played Christmas music from her cell phone music list. Another nurse brought in a bottle of wine and Popeye and Joe the Gimp respectfully declined. Esmeralda graciously accepted.

"Well, how about me?" Micko asked.

In unison, several voices answered, "Head wounds cannot be given alcohol or pain meds."

Miss Kitty arrived and sheepishly slid up to Joe the Gimp's bed. She whispered in Joe's ear for several moments and stepped back with a big smile on her face.

"Kitty says that Hannity's Manor is completely flooded, and the residents are being relocated to Red Cross operations in schools. The same for the Hanoi Hilton and the vets. Volunteers from the ASPCA on 92nd Street are collecting all of the animals, and a counselor from an outreach program has found her an SRO room next to mine," Joe said.

"Well, well, well. It seems that everything is turning out A-OK. I don't think the flooding affected the east side Mole People, but I wonder what will happen to the Morlock Nation?" Micko asked.

The Christmas party lasted for hours until Micko fell asleep to the song, "There'll be a Hot Time in the Old Town Tonight."

The after-work Christmas party was in full swing at The Bravest Bar at 700 Second Avenue on the east side of Manhattan. While Christmas was usually earmarked for family, many locals dropped by to enjoy the party, even if just to say hello and have a single drink. Many Manhattan companies did not close for the day, so travelers had a taste while waiting for their commute home. Since Penn Station was in such a mess, Grand Central Station was overcrowded. The nearby Bravest was the place to wait for the train.

Wanda was surprised at the turnout and had to get behind the bar and help out the overwhelmed bartenders. She and her husband Mick had been running this bar for over twenty years and loved every minute of it.

"Sanchez, come over here," she said.

"Si, señorita," a small Mexican man answered.

"Go down to the basement and hook up a fresh keg of Guinness. If there is not one there, bring one up from the sub-basement."

"Si."

Sanchez walked to the rear of the establishment behind the kitchen. There he lifted the large trap door to gain access to the steep stairs below. He walked to the delivery ramp leading up to the sidewalk and side alley, where the beer was delivered and stored. He didn't see any Guinness kegs, so he knew he would have to take the dumbwaiter lift down to the dark, cold sub-basement.

Sanchez looked around for a flashlight and found a small, cheap one sitting on a workbench. He hated taking the old lift down. He was afraid of it breaking and leaving him trapped in the dark.

Cautiously he operated the dumbwaiter down. He was pleased it went smoothly and he looked for the keg storage area. The walls were old cobblestoned relics from a long-ago era. Cold and damp, he felt a chill.

Suddenly, from the corner of his eye in the shadows he glimpsed a mob of small people scurrying past him and down a sewer hole. Initially, he thought they were children playing.

Sanchez ran to the sewer they had climbed down and flashed his light down the metal wall rungs. A ghoulish face appeared for a second and quickly disappeared into the darkness below.

The simple man became completely unhinged. He screamed in terror, bolted through the cobblestone alley, and went back to the lift. Panicking, Sanchez was pressing every button on the control panel, but the dumbwaiter wouldn't move.

"Help me!" he shrieked.

Wanda walked to the kitchen for some fresh limes when she heard Sanchez calling for help.

"Be quiet and get into the lift," she called down the shaft.

"Madre de Dio!" he cried out.

Mick came into the kitchen and asked, "What the hell is going on here?"

Wanda ignored him and pressed the green UP button on the dumbwaiter and instantly heard the electric motor engage and raise the lift.

When the ancient elevator came to a stop, the poor man ran into Wanda's arms, crying and babbling about seeing aliens in the sub-basement running through the sewers.

"Mick, you had better have a talk with these Mexicans and tell them not to smoke any pot while working here. We're running a business, not a day care center. If they want to get high and act like children, then let them do it on their own time."

"I'll change the keg myself, Wanda, just calm Sanchez down."

Mick went below and realized he must go farther below for the desired keg. When he arrived at the lower floor, he spotted the flashlight Sanchez had carried, lying on the floor. He picked it up and looked around. He saw the sewer cover askew and realized someone had been down there. He calmly put the cover in place, stacked two beer barrels on top, and sneered.

"Whoever is playing games down here will now have to exit by the East River," he said aloud to the empty basement.

The unanticipated move did not cause anarchy among the Morlocks. The underground dwellers merely moved from the west side of Manhattan to the east side. They had been survivalists for many generations and deep below the city streets, the Morlocks would thrive once again.

www.ingramcontent.com/pod-product-compliance
Lightning Source LLC
Chambersburg PA
CBHW051507170626
46811CB00002B/691